BEFORE SHE WAS TAKEN

The Killing Hour Book Two

MARGIE BENEDICT

For Kay Benedict Liscomb

Part I

MOONLIGHT SPILLS across the frayed mustard carpet to reach Nicki, splayed on her back atop the rock-hard mattress of her bed. The brightness wakes her as she had intended. At bedtime, Mother had lowered the shades, but Nicki had quietly raised them after she left.

The time is three in the morning. Her hands tingle as she rises and puts on her heavy blue hoodie over her pajamas. She crosses to the chair, trying not to look at the yellowed wallpaper with pictures of little girls in pigtails playing on a slide, on a swing set, in a sandbox, and splashing in a baby pool. However much Nicki grows—she turned sixteen last month—it feels like she's forever trapped inside the moments of childhood depicted on these four walls.

She picks up Cinderella, a large stuffed bear with one eye missing, and reaches under her skirt through the hole she slashed into her long ago. With the stuffing removed, the space serves as a hiding place for any cash she manages to steal, and for the treats she saves for Sadie. Nicki removes half of a Hershey's chocolate bar and pockets it before putting on her sneakers and tiptoeing to the door.

With practiced caution, she turns the knob, slips through the narrow opening, and silently closes the door behind her. She pauses to listen to Uncle's gruntlike snores from the room next to hers. It gives her some courage to confirm he's asleep. Unfortunately, she can't be certain about Mother, in the bedroom across the hall, who never makes a sound that can be heard outside her room.

Nicki proceeds to the stairs and descends them with delicate steps, careful to avoid the parts that creak the loudest. She's almost at the bottom and ready to congratulate herself, when the wood groans under her foot. Freezing in place, she listens for sounds of stirring.

After a minute passes without anyone coming, she decides it's safe to continue. Thankfully, the hall and kitchen have linoleum floors that allow her to cross quietly. The drawer, on the other hand, sticks to its frame and makes a horrible noise if she's not careful. She must open it for the flashlight, though, and she manages well enough. She'll worry about closing it later.

She takes a water bottle from the box by the counter before snatching the key to the shed from behind one of the shelves. Some time ago, she discovered where Uncle kept it by spying on him from inside the pantry.

Her last hurdle is the back door, so tight in its frame it has to be yanked open. It makes some noise and even rattles the house a bit, but it's too late to turn back now. She escapes outside and down the steps, where she pauses for a gulp of the brisk air scented with pine. A shiver skips down her spine at the sight of the moonlit trees, lurking around the edge of the property like rows of tall, spindly jailers.

She dashes across the carpet of pine needles to get to the shed, and lets herself in with the key, closing the door after her. Switching on the flashlight, she's careful not to aim it at the bed since no one likes to be woken with bright light in their eyes.

Four-year-old Sadie is curled under the blanket looking up at her. Her hair is matted and there's a dark smudge on her left cheek. She sucks on the tip of her thumb, with a filthy, threadbare rabbit missing most of its stuffing clutched under her arm.

Nicki sits on the mattress beside her and touches her hair. "Hey there," she whispers.

Sadie lowers her thumb. "Hey."

"I brought you a treat." Nicki takes out the chocolate bar.

Sadie sits up and leans against the wall. "Thank you."

"Should we have a tea party?"

Sadie nods.

Nicki arranges the rabbit and a stuffed dog with a monocle on either side of them. Recovering four plastic teacups piled in the corner, she sets them in front of everyone and pours a bit of water into the cups. "Sugar?"

"Yes, two please," Sadie says.

Nicki drops imaginary sugar cubes into her cup and turns to the rabbit. "Becca?"

"One half, please." Nicki provides the high-pitched voice of Becca the rabbit.

Pretending to struggle to break the cube in half, Nicki speaks in an aside to Sadie. "She only wants to make things difficult."

"I heard that," the rabbit voice replies.

"Mr. Fluffernutter doesn't need any. He doesn't like sweets," Sadie says regarding the dog.

"They, hem, interfere with my digestion." Nicki lends Mr. Fluffernutter a deep growly tone.

Sadie places a piece of her chocolate in front of Becca.

"I'd like half of that," the rabbit says.

"No!" Sadie says, laughing.

"Tomorrow let's take Becca to the salon and get her fur done," Nicki says.

"I went there yesterday!" Sadie does the rabbit voice. "Can't you tell?"

"Oh my, and a beautiful job they did too." Nicki winks at Sadie.

"Mr. Fluffernutter should get a pedicure," Sadie says.

"Hem, only if I may get the purple glitter polish," is Mr. Fluffernutter's response.

Sadie sips from her cup. "I want to see my mommy."

Nicki glances back toward the house. "Mother's sleeping now."

"Not her." Sadie makes a face. "My real mommy."

"She's your real mommy now. And he's your uncle."

Sadie shakes her head hard. Her face crumples and tears start to flow.

"Come here." Nicki moves everything out of the way and sits beside her holding the girl's hand in her lap. "You have to be patient. Things that are important take time."

"I miss her," Sadie whispers.

"I know. I'll take care of you. You have to trust me." But even as the words emerge from her lips, she hears the heavy shoes pounding down the back steps of the house and rushing toward them.

Chapter Two

REBECCA HURRIES toward Dev as he waits for the garage elevator.

"Hey there," she says, slowing abruptly, becoming all casual, like she hasn't been waiting in her white Honda Fit parked near the entrance, watching for his return from work.

He glances back, surprised at her appearance. "Oh, hi. How are you?"

"Great. It's my night off," she says.

"Have anything special planned?"

"Maybe." She tries for an enigmatic smile, which only causes him to look puzzled.

The elevator doors open and he waits while she enters first. Her gaze drinks him in as he presses the button for their mutual floor. A marketing exec at a high-tech company, he's meticulously turned out in dark slacks and a white button shirt that contrasts beautifully with his toffee-colored skin. No jacket or tie because this is Silicon Valley, not Wall Street. As the doors slide together, the sensation of their being alone in an enclosed space causes a prickle of excitement inside her.

"You remember that new wine club I told you about?" she says.

His eyes light up with interest. Since the time some months ago when he passed her in the hall carrying a case of premium California cabernet, she's been aware of his obsession.

"I got my first shipment three days ago. And I know I should let the bottles rest, but I couldn't resist opening the pinot. Russian River Valley. It's amazing." She ought to use more precise descriptors to impress him—*earthy* or *spicy* or *notes of barnyard*—but she's never gotten the hang of that and is certain she'll screw it up.

"Really? Remind me what club this is," he says.

"It's called… wait, don't take my word for it. I'd feel terrible if you joined and didn't like the wine. Our tastes might be different."

"True, I never like the stuff that gets high ratings from *The Wine and Truth Journal.*"

"Have you got a minute? You can come try it yourself."

He looks nervous at this point. No doubt it flashes across his mind that his girlfriend might not be thrilled by his interaction with this young, unattached neighbor. But the lure of wine is too strong. "Uh, sure, why not? Thanks."

They spill out of the elevator and he follows her into her living space. "Nice place," he says, glancing around. She's never been in his apartment but she assumes it's exactly the same, other than their decorating choices. Her furniture is only one step up from *college student,* but he shouldn't expect anything fancier from someone earning a pittance as a waitress. Although she does have some inherited income, it mostly goes toward paying the absurd cost of renting a measly one-bedroom unit in Silicon Valley.

The open bottle of pinot noir awaits them on the counter. She takes out two wide-bottom wineglasses and fills them a third of the way. Handing one to Dev, she clinks it with the other. "Cheers." Slipping into full connoisseur mode, she swirls the glass and sniffs the wine before sipping and swooshing it inside her mouth. She closes her eyes and parts her lips to breathe in and let the air open up the wine. Only then does she swallow and look at Dev, whose fathomless eyes are fixed on her.

"Have a seat?" She nods toward the couch, letting him settle there ahead of her. She brings the bottle along with her glass and sits right next to him, pinning him on one side with their arms nearly touching. He looks as if he'd like to switch to a chair, but doesn't want to seem rude.

Rebecca prompts Dev to talk about wine. While he waxes poetic regarding the optimum terroir for cab versus pinot, she wriggles out of the coat she has kept on until now. Underneath, she wears a short, ass-hugging black skirt and a lowcut silk camisole with no bra underneath. Quite accidentally of course, she pushes closer to Dev after tossing the coat behind the couch.

He loses his train of thought and compensates by slurping down the rest of his wine like lemonade on a hot day.

"So you like it?" she says.

"Love it."

It is, in fact, an absolutely delicious concoction that glides over the palette. It took many days of experimentation for her to identify a pinot noir that would be exactly to Dev's taste.

"Let me get you some more." She leans past him for the bottle and gives him a telescopic view of her breasts while she fills his glass. When she's done, she *unintentionally* loses her balance and falls into his lap. He grasps her waist to help her, which naturally leads to her arms wrapping around his neck. He's not the man to resist kissing her now, and the rest follows because, of course, *wine*. Besides, he must be thinking if he's going to get nailed for cheating, he may as well experience the full benefit of it.

The sex ends too quickly, which is both the good and bad of it. It's like the adrenalin rush of jumping off a cliff as opposed to the gentle, euphoric sensation of gliding to the bottom with wings.

They hold each other briefly afterward, while she questions her life choices. Eight months ago, she became a time traveler after being sparked by an unusual rock she encountered off the trail during a hike. At first she thought she was having unbelievably realistic dreams. But before long, she learned she could pick the moment she wanted to revisit simply by concentrating on it. Her time jumps ended naturally whenever she achieved a sense of completion or simply when she could no longer remain awake. She made up a name to describe the process—*mindcast*. Her body stayed home while her consciousness leapt backward to occupy younger versions of herself.

Through experimentation, she found that her actions in the past never changed anything in the present. It was as if an alternate time thread opened up… like there might be infinite possible variations. Mindcasting allowed her to experience some of these variations, without, fortunately, becoming stuck in any one of them. In the end she always returned to what she thought of as *real-time*.

It soon came to her how she could use this power to do things no one but she would ever know about or remember. If she seduced Dev during a mindcast, he would have no idea in real-time. She would have all the pleasure of fucking him, without any of the complications.

It took eleven jumps to perfect the method of seducing Dev. Since then, they had done it seventeen times using this exact scenario. Despite telling herself it was enough, she kept returning to this day like a glutton unable to forgo cheesecake at the end of each meal. Each time, remorse and disgust filled her afterward, but it wasn't sufficient to stop her from repeating the same act on the next night or the night after that. She imagines she's some sort of sex addict, but even more twisted because she craves that extra level of fervor that comes of his thinking this is the first time he's ever touched her in his life.

Escaping before the inevitable moment of extreme awkwardness, she begins her return journey through time. The inside of her head grows hot and her vision fades. But this time, instead of seeing only blackness, she pictures four-year-old Sadie as if through a shroud. An instant later her sister is gone, disappearing as she did outside their house nineteen years ago, when Rebecca was six and supposed to be watching her.

Chapter Three

WHEN REBECCA WAKES in the morning, she gets the sinking feeling she's overslept again. A glance at the time on her phone confirms she should've been at the wildlife refuge an hour ago.

Dammit. Her eyes used to pop open at eight every day, regardless of when she went to bed. But lately a feeling of lethargy has come over her. Since nothing else has changed in her life, it has to be related to the mindcasts. At first, she thought they only occupied a flicker of a second in real-time. Somewhere she'd read that dreams pass that quickly, and she had for some reason assumed her time travel worked similarly. But now she wonders if the mindcasts rob her of as much sleep as the number of hours she remains in the past.

She races through her shower and blasts her hair with the dryer at the maximum setting. Glad for her short cut that dries quickly, she only wishes she had more time to style it. A bit of gel tames it, at least.

After tossing on a cotton top and jeans, she calls Gary. "Hey, running late this morning. I'll be there in forty-five."

"Um, Rebecca, this is like the fifth time this month? Sarah already did a bunch of your assignments," Gary says.

"I'm really sorry. It won't happen again."

"You told me that last week. I think you should take a break, like, get your shit together?"

Get your shit together. That stings. "I'm a volunteer, for god's sake." It feels like he's expecting a lot from a free employee.

"Yeah, no kidding, but we still need to be able to count on you."

"Please give me another chance."

"Let's give it till after the holidays? Call me then if you're ready to commit to a schedule." He ends their conversation before she can protest any further.

She slumps down onto the nearest chair, thinking of the animals she's helped care for since she began volunteering three years ago. Angus the barn owl who loves to be rinsed off with the hose on hot days. Sir Lancelot the gray fox, an expert climber. The Bobbsey Twin bobcats that wrangle with each other constantly. Even Jesse the king snake with his beautiful orange markings. She can't imagine how she'll get through the next two months without seeing them.

Eventually her empty stomach drives her out for coffee and a sesame bagel at Mathilda Café. She settles into her favorite little table by the window, where the bright sunlight warms her. It's diverting at least to watch people passing on the sidewalk, enjoying the Bay Area weather that feels more like summer than fall. When she's finished eating, she too sets off for a walk along the streets of the nearest residential neighborhood.

After several blocks, she notices a white van creeping past a house where children are playing outside. Most likely it's a service vehicle looking for a particular address, but just in case, Rebecca takes a picture of the back of it, making sure to get a clear image of the license plate. She often photographs suspicious-looking cars, and pedestrians who linger too long or stare too intently at houses and the families living in them.

She organizes the pictures by street and date and stores them in files on her computer. If a serious crime or an abduction occurs in the area, she'll bring the photos to the attention of local law enforcement. Once a murder did happen and she got in touch with Freddie, a detective who worked on her sister's disappearance. He took copies of her pictures and later told her they helped in solving the case, though she believed he only said that to be kind.

Rebecca knows her habit is weird and probably won't make a difference. But if it ever leads to even a single success… to a crime being thwarted, a killer being apprehended, or a child being found… it will have been worth any amount of time she put into it. Sadie might've been saved if someone had noticed a suspicious vehicle trolling the streets of Windlake and snapped a picture, or at least made a note of its license.

When she returns to her apartment and downloads the photo of the van, she glances through the other images in her collection. It occurs to her she could make a collage out of them, particularly the older photos that aren't likely to be of use anymore. She would have to blacken any identifying information, like license plates, house numbers, and people's faces. Maybe give it a title, like *Fear and Suspicion in Suburbia* or *Diary of a Madwoman*.

During the rest of the afternoon, she solves logic puzzles, a hobby she's enjoyed since high school. She's always had a knack for them, a skill that must've come from her father, a mathematics professor at U.C. Berkeley. But unlike him, she decided not to pursue a career based on numbers. She decided not to pursue a career in anything, in fact.

She eats the leftover Thai takeout for an early dinner before rushing out to her job at Pythonella, making certain to arrive on time, especially since she's been late for three out of four of her last shifts. After losing her volunteer position this morning, she's determined to hang onto her one actual, paying job.

But as the night continues, she finds her attention wandering. Somehow she writes down the garlic pasta with Cajun cauliflower only to have the customer later insist she asked for the basil pasta with roast chicken. All the ladies in their large group were talking at once when Rebecca took the order. They ought to shush up if they expect to get the meal they want.

Then ten minutes after that debacle, she delivers an order for two to the wrong couple. Worse, they don't notice immediately, causing the food to be left on the table for several minutes before Rebecca is called back. This results in two wasted dinner entrees that can't be re-delivered, and two customers unhappy to have to wait another twenty minutes for their food.

At the end of the evening, Joanna the owner and head chef calls Rebecca into her private office that somehow always smells of rosemary, despite the myriad of scents produced in the kitchen next door. "Got something on your mind lately?" Joanna says.

"No, I'm fine." Rebecca decides her wisest course is to pretend everything is normal.

"So this is the best we can expect from you from now on?"

"I thought I did okay."

"*Okay* is not the way we ever want anyone to describe Pythonella. How many people do you think will eat here, if the reviewer says the food is *okay*, the ambiance, *okay*, and the service, *okay*?"

"I'll try to do better."

"You cost us money tonight."

"Take it out of my tips."

"I doubt you earned the tips to cover it."

This is close to the truth, especially since her distracted behavior has led to stingy rewards.

"I'm going to cut one of your work days. Jaqueline will take Saturdays."

"I get my best tips on Saturdays. How about Thursday?"

"You show me what *outstanding* service you can provide, and we'll see about getting Saturday back for you," she says. "Now go on home. Get some rest. You look like you need it."

It's true she's been a lousy employee. Joanna has every right to cut down her work week. But it hits her all at once how much she hates this job. That clenched feeling inside her stomach isn't coming from the thought of losing a day's work, but from heavy disappointment that she didn't get fired outright.

"I quit," she says.

Joanna raises her eyebrows. "You can't do that. I can't replace you that fast."

"Try Jaqueline," she says before leaving the office and walking straight out of the restaurant, where the crisp night air cools her face and the tension slips from her joints.

It isn't until she's halfway across the parking lot that she notices a small red Kia parked on the right side. She doesn't recognize it as belonging to any of the other employees. The streetlamp above the car illuminates a man in the driver's seat. His profile seems familiar to her and there are marks around his neck. A tattoo. It's too dark to tell if it depicts an eagle with wings spread on both sides. But it might.

A spike of adrenalin propels Rebecca to her Honda. As soon as she's inside, she locks all the doors and checks her rear view. The man is getting out of the Kia. She turns her key, the engine cranks, but the car doesn't start. *Come on, come on.* Checking the mirror again, she glimpses the man stepping in the direction of her car. A second turn of the key, the engine cranks. *Go, go, go.* It finally starts and she throws it into reverse, hits the gas, brakes hard, shifts forward, and careens out of the parking lot, right into the street without checking who's coming. A car squeals behind her and honks as she speeds away.

The man who got out of the Kia had white hair. Bray Reamer's hair was light brown when he was sent to prison. But that was a long time ago.

Chapter Four

FOR THE NEXT FEW DAYS, Rebecca alternates between long walks and working on her collection of math puzzles. Since her mother left her an inheritance that came from her grandfather, a commercial property developer, she doesn't exactly need to race into a new job.

Sadie has begun appearing in her dreams again. When Rebecca wakes, though, she usually can't remember anything that happened aside from having seen her sister. Except for one recent dream, where Sadie arrived at her apartment all grown up, insisting her so-called disappearance was nothing more than a product of Rebecca's imagination.

By the end of the fourth day, she craves another mindcast rendezvous with Dev. It's in her thoughts when she leaves her apartment to pick up dinner from Hola's, and finds herself face to face with Dev and his girlfriend in the hall.

"Rebecca, hi," he says, seeing her approach. "Have you met my girlfriend, Lisa?"

Lisa is a striking woman of Asian heritage, with long sleek black hair and an irresistible dimpled smile. Caught off guard, Rebecca hopes her face reveals no hint of the lust that filled her only seconds ago while she was imagining Lisa's boyfriend having sex with her.

"Oh right, Dr. Sheng, isn't it?" Rebecca says, recalling that the woman has somehow already qualified as a pediatrician though they look the same age.

"Call me Lisa." She flashes her killer smile as the elevator arrives and she and Dev wait for Rebecca to enter first.

"Rebecca works at Pythonella," Dev says.

"Oh, I love that place! Are you the chef?" Lisa says.

"I don't work there anymore." Rebecca leaves Lisa to imagine she might've been the chef. No reason to admit she got fired for failing at a job anyone can learn to do passably well in about two weeks.

"Are you starting your own restaurant?" Lisa says.

Rebecca shrugs. "We'll see." As if this is an actual possibility.

The elevator doors open as Dev tells her, "We'd love to eat there."

She almost snorts, picturing slabs of burnt toast and undercooked eggs artfully arranged on decorative plates. "You'll be the first to know." She rushes past them to the street, but can't resist glancing back. Pressed together, Dev and Lisa stare into each other's eyes with lovesick expressions. They're so ridiculously gorgeous and exotic, they might as well be rehearsing for the role of this year's celebrity golden couple. Rebecca feels like retching.

Seeing them together has effectively destroyed her appetite for sex with Dev tonight. Instead, she spends the evening eating her chicken mole in front of the TV, re-watching the Harry Potter films starting from the first until she falls asleep in the middle of the third.

In the morning she gets a text from her father's wife asking if she's coming to their barbecue this afternoon. They invited her two weeks ago but she never answered. She's about to make an excuse when she remembers she has something she wants to discuss with him. She texts back accepting the invitation before she can change her mind again.

Rebecca and her father barely get along. She used to blame it on his being one of those people who don't connect well with children. Someone who had to be talked into having them by her mother. But then, in the seven years since she left his home at age eighteen, he married for the second time and his twelve-year-younger wife promptly gave birth to two boys—Tyler who's now five, and Kevin who is three. Rebecca has seen the way he dotes on them, nothing like what she recalls from her own childhood.

She's half an hour past the start time when she reaches their house in Berkeley. The shrieks of the boys playing in the backyard draw her to the side gate. Part of her misses this home where she grew up after her mother died. It's early November, and the gingko trees are splayed out like golden sheaves, while the Chinese pistache in the corner flaunts a full circlet of burnished red leaves. Despite the appearance of fall, temperatures still hover in the seventies, typical for California this time of year.

A dog that looks part German Shephard, part Husky, barks and dashes toward her.

"Scratch!" her father calls out. "No barking!"

Rebecca holds out her hand allowing the dog to sniff. "New family member?" she says as her father approaches.

They give each other a fleeting hug. "We got her six months ago," he says. "Has it been that long?" He's wearing his relaxing-at-home uniform, a gray T-shirt and khaki pants with enough pockets to accommodate a small toolbox worth of supplies.

"I thought you never wanted a dog." She spent the desolate nights following her mother's death wishing for one to share her bed.

He nods at his oldest. "Tyler was relentless."

Rebecca waves across the lawn at her father's wife cooking hamburgers on the barbecue. "Hey there, Marie."

"Hi, glad you could make it."

Unsurprisingly, Rebecca detects a rebuke in her tone. Probably for the two-weeks-late response to her text, the half-hour-late arrival at the house, and other offenses Rebecca isn't even aware she committed.

The dog rejoins the two boys, who are tackling each other over a ball. "Hey, kiddos, where's my hug?" Rebecca calls out.

They race to be first to squeeze her around the waist.

"Who's going to toss me the ball?" Rebecca plays catch with her stepbrothers and the dog while her father helps Marie prepare the burgers. Kevin, with a recent buzzcut that makes his head look rounder, says, "Look, Dad built us a treehouse!"

"Oh yeah? Can you show me?" She's seen it before but Kevin is young enough not to remember the last time she came.

He takes her hand and leads her to the tree, while Tyler races past them, swinging up the ladder to be first into the structure. The disappointed Kevin follows with Rebecca behind him. She peers at the two boys seated cross-legged inside. "This is so cool." Envy burns her up inside. All she and Sadie asked for was a rope swing but her father put it off with lame excuses. She forces that remembrance aside, smiling as the boys display the toys that live in the hideout.

"Lunch is ready," Marie says.

Tyler and Kevin jump up and scramble down the ladder as soon as Rebecca gets out of the way. They gather at the picnic table, where the food has already been laid out.

"Where are the hot dogs?" Tyler says.

"You told me you wanted burgers," Marie says.

"I want a hot dog!" He pouts.

"Me too," says Kevin, though clearly his heart isn't in it.

"Well this is what we have," Marie says.

Tyler pushes his plate to the ground and the dog wastes no time in snatching up the meat. "Scratch ate my hamburger!" Tyler looks like he regrets it now.

The parents exchange exasperated looks. "We don't have any hot dogs," Marie says.

"I'll get some," Rebecca's father says.

"No." Marie's voice is sharp. "I know what kind he likes. I won't be long." She leaves right away, clearly anxious to avoid being stuck alone with her stepdaughter.

Rebecca is thinking how fast she would've been sent up to her room with nothing to eat if she behaved like this at Tyler's age. But no one has a harsh word to say to him. The boys shove in handfuls of potato chips before returning to the yard to toss the ball for Scratch, leaving Rebecca and her father alone at the table.

"Beer?" he says.

"Sure."

He opens two cold ones from the cooler and hands one across to her.

"Nice beard," she says. He was cleanshaven last time she saw him. "It's kind of reddish."

"Like this used to be." He rubs the top of his mostly bald

head. "You look a little tired. Are you still working at that restaurant?"

"I quit a few days ago."

His thick eyebrows raise up. He never wanted her to be a waitress. "So what are you doing?"

"Nothing, Dad. Absolutely nothing."

"Seriously? If you're not working, you could at least take some classes."

It's their age-old argument. "Classes in what? I'll find another job soon enough."

"As a waitress." He says it exactly as he might say *hooker* or *drug dealer*.

"Maybe. It's a perfectly good profession. You act like it's beneath me."

"If you were happy being a waitress, I wouldn't say anything about it."

"How do you know if I'm happy or not?"

"Tell me, then. Are you happy being a waitress?"

He knows she can't lie to him. She swigs from her beer.

"You were so good at math," he says. "You should do something that challenges you."

"I guess I ought to become a math professor like you."

"Why not, if you have the ability? You'll never know unless you go to college. There's a lot of different things you can do with a math degree."

"It's too late for me."

"Don't be crazy. You're twenty-five. You've got all the time in the world."

"Do I?" She wraps her hands around the weeping bottle. "Do you ever think about her anymore?"

There isn't any question who *her* is. "Of course I do," he answers gruffly.

"Then I don't know how you can…"

"What? Lead a happy life? Maybe you'd rather I acted like your mother."

"That's a terrible thing to say." Her mother had taken pills. It might've been suicide, or it might've been an accident. Either way it came to the same thing.

She lowers her voice. "I think I saw him the other day."

"Saw who?"

"You know. Reamer."

Her father stares at her.

"When I was leaving work, he was in a car watching me."

"Why would he do that?"

"I don't know. Maybe he blames us for the long sentence he got."

"If he did it, he knows he got off easy," her father says. "I'm sure you imagined it was him in the car. He lives in Fresno now."

"Only a few hours to drive here from there."

He takes a long slurp from his bottle. "Are you still seeing that therapist?"

Frustration fills her. "You never believe anything I say. You never have."

"That isn't true."

Kevin wails and she glances back to see him flat on his butt. "Tyler pushed me!" he cries out.

"I shouldn't have come." She stands up.

"You're letting him win, you know," her father says.

"What do you mean?"

"He got two of our family already. Don't let him take another."

"What can I do about it?"

"Everything." He rises and goes to his sons.

Chapter Five

REBECCA LEAVES her father's house before Marie returns from the market. She should've known better than to go there. Seeing him just makes the grief resurface. Maybe when her brothers grow older, she can have a better relationship with them, but not if their parents' spoiling turns them into entitled adults.

After returning home, she pours herself a glass of wine and sits on the couch, staring at nothing. Her life is shit. She has alienated the few friends she once had, lost her job that helped pay the bills, and been put on leave from the volunteer work that brought her some happiness. She has a lover who is literally a phantom. Her father and his family will probably want nothing further to do with her following today's performance.

She knows deep down that he gave her good advice regarding college. It could be exactly what she needs to get her life back on track, if only she could motivate herself to get started. But the to-do list overwhelms her. Researching college programs… deciding which career track interests her the most... filling out and submitting applications... and possibly having to arrange a move if the place that accepts her is too far. She can't wrap her head around any of this, particularly the moving part. These days she feels as if she's a rare creature whose travels on earth are not meant to involve distance, but time. All because of the average-looking stone that threw a spark at her. She had thought little of it then, until the mindcasts began. Even now, she can't be certain the two events are related, but her instinct says they are. She wishes she had taken the rock home with her. It would be impossible for her to ever locate it again, particularly since she encountered it off-trail.

She isn't sure how long she sits in a vegetative state before hunger finally drives her to the kitchen. Not feeling like going out or even ordering in, she prepares an English muffin with melted cheese to accompany the bit of leftover Mexican food she still has in the fridge. She opens a fresh bottle of Syrah and drinks two glasses with her meal.

When she eventually gets into bed, she's planning on reading herself to sleep. Instead, her thoughts turn to Dev. What harm could there be in paying him a visit in the unalterable past and seducing him? It's not as though she forces him into anything; he enjoys himself as much as she does.

After ten more minutes of rationalization, she sets her thoughts to the time and day when she always meets up with him. Before long, she feels the familiar burning inside her head, and the dizzying sensation of flipping back in time. She follows the script as usual, pretending to accidentally run into him outside the elevator, telling him about the pinot noir, and inviting him into her apartment. They sit on the couch, drinking, while he drones on about wine production methods.

Part of her wants so much to be with him, especially after

the wrenching disappointments of the last few days. But another part is watching as if outside her own body—which is, in fact, a fairly accurate description of her situation, given that her present-day mind has jumped back into a little-bit-younger version of herself.

But just as she prepares to reach over and pour more wine for him—starting the all-important seduction phase of this whole charade—she suddenly feels as if she's in the middle of a poorly written romance novel, with her as the desperate, insecure heroine.

Laughter bubbles out of her, building up, making her whole body shake while tears sprout from her eyes.

Dev is perplexed, maybe wondering if he's the oblivious butt of her private joke. "Um, did I say something?"

"It's just that… the wine… the situation… you… me…" She loses control as her laughter morphs into sobbing.

"Are you okay? Maybe I should go."

It takes a moment for her to manage to speak again. "No, I just… I think I really need someone to talk to."

"You have a girlfriend you can call?"

She shakes her head. "Pathetic, I know. My life is completely fucked up and it's my own fault. It all started when I was six. I'm a terrible person."

"No, you're not. You're very nice." He checks his phone.

"I was supposed to be watching my little sister. She was only four. But I ditched her to play with my friend. Sadie wandered off to the front yard by herself." She has to gulp a few times before she can finish this. "That was the last time I ever saw her."

She's not sure what to expect. She hasn't told anyone about Sadie in years. He's just staring down at his hands saying nothing.

"I still don't know what happened to her. There's a guy… I think he did it. But there was zero evidence. Two years after she disappeared, my mother OD'ed on Ambien."

All she wants is some comforting words and a warm hug. Reassurance that she did nothing any other six-year-old would not do. A pat on her back and a kind voice telling her things will get better.

He gets up from the couch. "Sorry about what happened. I wish I could stay and talk about it. But I'm meeting my girlfriend in a half hour. I have to go."

Her mouth falls open in disbelief. *Meeting my girlfriend…* Rebecca knows for a fact that Lisa is at a conference in Chicago right now. It's why she chose this day.

When he was fucking her, he never had to run off and meet his girlfriend.

He slinks across the room and out the door, pausing only to twist the knife with his final words. "Thanks for the wine. It's not my style, though."

When the door is shut behind him, she takes his glass and flings it at the wall. It shatters into a thousand pieces, dripping wine like blood onto her floor.

Chapter Six

REBECCA KNOWS what she has to do. She's known ever since she first gained the ability to transmit her consciousness back in time. Fear has kept her from it, though. Fear of learning that Sadie's suffering was even worse than she could've imagined. Fear that she lacks the fortitude to handle the horror of what her sister faced.

But her life has hit rock bottom and she has nothing more to lose. Her father's words ring inside her: *You're letting him win… don't let him take another*. He had been speaking metaphorically about the ways she was failing at life. But he could equally well have been referring to other possible victims. Bray Reamer finished serving his sentence six months ago. What if he took another child?

Nothing was ever proven against him. A year after Sadie disappeared, police arrested him for selling marijuana he cultivated in the backyard of the house he was renting. When they searched inside, they found child pornography. He was selling that too.

He lived a mile from their house and he was the strongest

suspect the police ever identified. When he tried to skip bail and escape to Mexico, he was caught and brought back to stand trial for drug and child pornography trafficking charges.

They searched inside and out but never found any evidence of Sadie having been at his house. A whole year had passed by the time of his arrest, giving him plenty of opportunity to obliterate any evidence of her. The FBI dug up the yard and brought in dogs to sniff everywhere, but still nothing turned up. Again and again, they interrogated Reamer without his ever admitting having anything to do with Sadie's abduction. With no confession and no proof, law enforcement had to drop the case against him.

He served seventeen years for his other crimes, but now he's out, and Rebecca is afraid he might be stalking her.

After her morning coffee, she takes down the Sadie box and unfolds the newspaper article in which Reamer's arrest was reported. It contains a bleary, black and white photograph, which she raises closer to her eyes. Could this be the man she saw in the restaurant parking lot? She can't be certain—it was dark and she didn't get a direct view of him.

Though she would much rather not, she tries to commit his face to memory. The odd choice of where to part his hair, too far to the right, almost like he meant to do a combover but he had too much hair for that. The plump nose and thin lips. The tattoo of an eagle reaching from behind to encircle his neck with its wings. That alone should be enough to identify him if he doesn't wear something to cover it up, and hasn't had it removed.

She sets the article aside and opens the photo album. Her mother took many pictures of Sadie from birth to four years, more than she took of Rebecca. Sadie sleeping in her crib…

with chocolate cake smeared on her face at her first birthday... half-buried in a pile of leaves... on a sled with their father in Lake Tahoe. There had been videos too, many of them, but these were all gone. Her mother destroyed them, saying that each time she watched one, it was like someone reaching into her chest and pulling out her beating heart, and yet she couldn't stop herself.

Rebecca thinks of this as she comes to the photo of her and Sadie in their pajamas, hugging each other tight with the Christmas tree behind them. It's too much for her and she has to close the album.

You're letting him win. She may not be able to beat him but she could at least mount a challenge. Through some miracle, she has gained an ability that may be unique in the world. It suddenly feels unbelievable that she's waited this long to use it for good. On the contrary, she's wasted it in the worst possible manner.

She'll take the first step today, she decides. This calls for putting a little effort into her appearance for a change. She dresses in her black straight leg jeans, a cream-colored blouse, and her fitted, green jacket. She styles her hair and dabs on lip gloss and eye-liner before setting out in her Honda Fit.

Her hands are clammy against the steering wheel as she drives toward Windlake underneath a solid bank of gray clouds. She expects they'll burn off by noon, as they generally do, though California is in desperate need of rain.

The last time she saw the house she was eight years old. By then her parents were divorced and her father had purchased the home in Berkeley. Her mother showed consideration in choosing to die while Rebecca was with her dad for the weekend. The timing was why she never believed the death was accidental. Well, this and one other reason. Her mother had stopped writing after Sadie was taken, and sometime before she died, she destroyed every copy—electronic and paper—of the one novel she'd completed, which had never been published. It still caused a deep ache inside Rebecca that her mother had chosen to eradicate this deeply personal thing she had created instead of leaving it for her daughter to savor as an adult, as her one remaining connection to her lost mother. At times it was hard not to hate her for what seemed like needlessly cruel and selfish actions, but she would remind herself to blame it instead on the sickness that had come over her mother.

Her father didn't bring her back to Windlake after that, figuring no good could come of Rebecca returning to the place where she'd experienced so much tragedy. He moved her toys, books and clothing to his house, before selling everything her mother owned, placing the proceeds into a trust since she was only eight.

Rebecca lets the GPS guide her to her former home. The freeway isn't crowded at this time, and after a while, she notices a small red car behind her, reminding her of the Kia that was parked at the restaurant. At first she shrugs it off as paranoia, then ten minutes later when it's still following her, she tries to glimpse the person in the driver's seat. But the sunlight reflecting off the front windshield makes it impossible to see inside the vehicle.

The driver maintains the same distance, even when Rebecca reduces her speed. After going another fifteen minutes with the car continuing to shadow her, she takes the next exit. To her great relief, the driver speeds past her on the freeway instead of following her.

Pulling up to a pump at the nearest gas station, she lowers her forehead on the steering wheel. She needs to pull herself together. Plenty of people own red cars, and quite possibly none of them belong to Bray Reamer. Even if it *was* him… she can't let him rattle her. Everything depends on her ability to keep a cool head.

After filling her tank, she returns to the freeway and listens to her favorite wildlife podcast until reaching her exit. The GPS guides her to her former home, but when she pulls up in front, she can't believe it's the place where she grew up, though the address is printed right there on the mailbox.

Before getting out, she leans across the seat to stare through the passenger window. In her memory, their house had wood siding painted gray, and a brown shake roof. Now the building is blue stucco with a red tile roof, white trim and a burgundy door. But the worst of it is, the majestic California oak that once stretched across their front lawn is gone.

Whenever she dreams of her childhood home, it's like a black and white Edward Gorey etching, with curved and crisscrossing branches making a jigsaw puzzle of the house behind them. Though its mood was somber and mysterious, she preferred it a thousand times to this thing it has become, a fourth of July centerpiece in Happy Town, USA.

The neighborhood has changed as well. Two new houses sandwich her old home, where once a weed-infested field surrounded their property. Across the street, a line of identical residences in garish shades has taken the place of a modest ranch house. Goats often grazed in its overgrown front yard.

On the positive side, it's hard to imagine a child being kidnapped here without anyone noticing.

Rebecca emerges from her car and approaches the house. A child in the back lets out the kind of playful cry she and Sadie would make when they ran through the sprinklers. She rings the bell and waits until shoes tap across the floor inside and the door comes open. A harried young mother holding a toddler against her hip looks at her with annoyance. Though it's not even eleven, the woman's eyes already wear a *get-me-out-of-here* glint. But Rebecca pretends not to notice and smiles at the child, causing her to turn away and smother her face against her mother's armpit.

"Sorry to bother you," Rebecca says, "but I used to live here and I was wondering if I could take a quick look inside. You know, for old time's sake."

A boy of about four-years-old walks up behind his mother and latches onto her leg.

"I'm busy, as you can see. I thought you were someone else." After this explanation of why she opened the door to a stranger, she starts to close it.

"My name is Rebecca Danser. My sister and I lived here when we were quite young."

The woman pauses to squint at her. "Danser…? Oh my god. It was your sister who…" She lays a protective hand on her boy as if danger might be lurking nearby.

"That's right. It would mean a lot to me if I could look around."

"Of course, I'm so sorry. Come in." She moves aside for Rebecca. "The realtor told us. They have to disclose that, even though it's been a long time."

"It didn't bother you?"

"It didn't seem that… whoever did it… would still be hanging around here. And the neighborhood has changed a lot. Right? I think it was more rural."

"Yeah, it wasn't anything like it is now." Rebecca hopes she finds this statement reassuring. She follows the woman and her kids into the kitchen, drawn by the heavy aroma of brownies in the oven. Somehow it conveys a feeling of home and family, though her own mother tended to burn everything she tried to bake.

Noticing Rebecca's confusion on glancing around, the woman says, "We're the third owners since your family moved out. All of us remodeled to some extent. I think we did the most. New appliances, cupboards, counters, floors, everything."

"It looks nice," Rebecca says. Like a page out of *House Beautiful*. Not like what she remembers of their old kitchen, where her mother always complained about the peeling floors, one electric burner that didn't work, and the stains on the countertops.

They continue to the room in the back, where their family had spent most of their time.

"New carpeting and paint," the mother says.

Her little boy, growing more courageous, approaches Rebecca. "Do you like dinosaurs?"

"My favorite is triceratops. Do you have one?"

He brightens and bounds up the stairs.

The opening to the backyard has been changed to French doors, but she can still picture her mother at the glass watching as they played outside. Now there's a gated swimming pool and a fancy play structure, but then they had a blow-up pool, a sandbox, and a short plastic slide.

She turns back, about to give up on the idea that there is anything left of her family here, when her gaze shifts to a familiar sight. "You kept the stone fireplace."

"Oh yes, we love it." The mother bounces the baby, who is starting to squawk.

Rebecca drops down on the floor beside it and turns on her phone flashlight. A timer buzzes in the kitchen.

"My brownies." The mother rustles out of the room.

Rebecca finds what she's looking for. *R & S*, their first name initials that they scratched with a sharp rock onto a dark stone on the right side. The *S* is barely legible because Sadie had insisted on doing hers. Rebecca touches the letter, squeezing her eyes shut, trying to picture her sister crouched there beside her as she was on that day.

"Whatcha doing?" The boy runs toward her carrying a box.

She shuts off the flashlight and sits on the floor as he dumps out his toys beside her. "Triceratops." He raises a large plastic specimen.

While he names each dinosaur, his mother brings them brownies and the toddler girl joins them on the floor, preferring to chew on a brontosaurus head. When Rebecca finishes eating, she thanks the woman, compliments the boy on his collection, and leaves the house grateful for this reminder of family connection. Seeing her former home has strengthened her resolve to move forward with her plan, which was exactly as she'd hoped.

She has another visit to pay while she's here, one that's difficult but necessary. Earlier she verified the directions—a right turn at the end of this street, then straight for three quarters of a mile, then a left onto Willow Lane. Reamer's former house sits at the end.

She drives slowly, paying attention to the terrain. The route is mainly flat, with a gentle uphill following the first turn, and a slight downhill preceding Willow. A narrow sidewalk hugs the road on one side for most of the way. A little girl could manage this walk without venturing into the street or tiring too much.

Rebecca parks near Reamer's former rental and gets out

of her car to survey the street, which is still relatively undeveloped. A field borders the house on the far side. Overall, the place—recently painted with a new roof—looks much nicer than she remembers. Rose bushes with fresh red, yellow, and pink blossoms line the walkway, filling the air with their enticing scent. By contrast, the one time Rebecca came to this house, sitting in the back of her mother's car, she thought it reeked of decay. Maybe that was simply a case of her projecting her thoughts onto the smell of the place.

Lost in memory, she doesn't notice the steps approaching behind her until the man is close. "What're you doin' here?" he says in a grating voice.

Her breath catches in her throat as she spins around. Bray Reamer lurks behind her, easily identifiable from the still-vibrant eagle tattoo surrounding his neck. His hair has gone white, as she guessed, and his face is flushed and leathery, with deep lines across his forehead. Compared to her memory, he's gained weight, which only makes him more imposing.

Before she can run, he grasps her arm.

"Let me go!" She tries to pull away but he tightens his grip.

"Why're you here?"

"Why are you following me?"

"You still think I did it," he says.

"You're hurting me!"

He releases her arm. "Want you to know I never touched her. Never kidnapped her. You got it all wrong."

A door opens across the road, and an elderly man steps out, holding his phone. "Are you all right, miss?" he calls out.

"I'm goin' now," Reamer says. "I didn't hurt her. That's not me. Never wanted to hurt anybody."

Rebecca isn't sure whether his remark refers to her or Sadie.

With his head lowered, he speed-walks toward his red Kia, parked near the intersection.

"Should I call the police, miss?" the neighbor says.

She could accuse Reamer of assault for the way he'd gripped her arm. But dealing with the police and providing a witness account will tie up her time. She can't put off what she needs to do any longer. "No, I'm all right," she says.

"You sure? Can't be too careful."

"I'm sure. Thanks for your help."

She waits until Reamer is gone before getting into her Honda. Driving back, her thoughts are full of the encounter. It was incredibly disturbing to confirm he's been watching her... following her even. And yet, the confrontation strengthened her resolve instead of weakening it. With him hanging around, it's all the more urgent she go back in time and find out the truth.

As determined as she is, however, she has to entertain the possibility that if she's killed in the past, that may truly be the end of her. The death of her former self could prevent her mind from returning to real-time.

Which is why her first action on arriving home is to write a letter to her father. It seems unlikely, but what if her body is still capable of functioning? He might have her connected to a machine to keep her alive. This is the last thing she wants. It would be a complete waste of his money, and might even give him hope where there would be none.

She dates the letter two years earlier so it doesn't appear she was able to predict she might end up as a vegetable. Her instructions are that she is not to be kept alive through artificial means. If she is unable to communicate her wishes or even form a coherent thought, then he must pull the plug as quickly as possible.

She fervently hopes this doesn't happen, because she's not certain she can trust him to honor her wishes. Also, without witnesses, the document is unlikely to be valid in any court of law. But it's better than doing nothing. She signs the letter, *Love, Rebecca*, which is the only reference she makes to her feelings for him. He and she are alike in this way. Stoic but steadfast. Bound to each other forever in grief, though he does a better job of masking it.

With this task out of the way, she makes herself two frozen waffles topped with real maple syrup for dinner. It's what she would request for her last meal on death row.

Later, thinking of Reamer, she checks to make sure she bolted the front door in addition to locking it. He clearly knows where she lives and could easily slip into the building while a resident is coming or going. People are careless about that. The real deterrent is the camera at the entrance. If he didn't care whether he was filmed or not, he most likely would've already broken in instead of following her about in his car. On the other hand, the man didn't appear rational so it's best to take at least the minimum of precautions.

When she finally settles into her bed, she focuses on the day that Sadie disappeared. It takes a long time for her to reach a sufficiently calm state of mind, but at last she answers the call of her six-year-old self, whose childhood ended that day as surely as did her sister's.

Part II

Chapter Seven

AFTER UNCLE CAUGHT Nicki sneaking out to the shed, he and Mother went back to keeping her locked in her room all the time except for meals and bathroom.

With nothing else to occupy herself, she does her schoolwork. She's not allowed to attend school because Mother thinks the other children would be a bad influence. But a few years ago, she begged Mother to buy her textbooks so she could still achieve a high school education and maybe even apply to college someday. At first Mother resisted and mocked her ambitions. But then one day in a used bookstore, Mother happened to spot a few decrepit volumes that were dirt cheap, maybe even free, and she brought them home. After Nicki began doing the lessons, she became less agitated and more cooperative, and Mother came to understand the benefits of allowing her to continue. From then on, Mother and Uncle would pick up textbooks, classic novels, short stories, and essays for her whenever they could find them for practically nothing.

She is highly motivated to excel in all her subjects,

because Mother eventually relented and told her she might allow her to apply to college after she turns eighteen—less than two years from now. She longs to be able to leave someday, despite the barrage of warnings from both of them regarding the dangers that exist beyond the confines of their house. Nicki knows little of the world, other than what she's been able to glean from reading, watching old films, and listening to conversations between Mother and Uncle, who both have jobs outside the house.

Today, just as she's cracking open her book on English composition, she hears the turn of the lock in her door. Mother lets herself in.

"Do you have a minute?" Mother, with her breathy, childish little voice, starts many of their conversations this way. It feels like cruel mockery, given that Nicki has all the minutes in the world, with not one single pressing matter to occupy her time.

"Sure." Nicki smiles like she's happy to see her, hopeful to regain her privileges.

Mother sits on the bed. "You've had some time to consider what you did wrong."

Nicki turns her chair to face her. "Yes, Mother."

"You might think I'm too strict, but the rules are there to keep you from harm. You can't be sneaking about in the dead of night. There could be wild animals, and all kinds of dangerous things out there."

Nicki wants to say, *Well, what about Sadie, all alone in the shed? Who is watching out for her?* But she knows this will just make Mother angry, and then there will be months more of lockup.

"I'm ready to give you another chance if you promise not to break the rules again."

"You'll stop locking my door?"

"Yes. Except at night, or when Uncle and I are both going to be out."

"I promise, Mother. I won't misbehave again."

She holds Nicki's gaze a moment longer before rising. "Let's watch a movie."

Nicki follows her into the hall and glances across at the door to Mother's bedroom. Most of the time she leaves it fully closed and locked, but today she's been careless and left it ajar. This could be Nicki's only chance for weeks or months to get her hands on an item she desperately needs that's kept inside the room.

Masking her excitement, she continues down the stairs after Mother, who pauses outside the TV room. "You pick," she says. "I'll get the snacks."

Nicki goes to the bookcase that holds their massive collection of old films on cassette, many of them westerns, including every feature starring Clint Eastwood. They've watched them over and over on their ancient VCR that never breaks down, despite Nicki wishing every day for lightning to strike it. Then maybe she could talk Mother into getting TV service instead, which, according to the movies they watch, every family except hers seems to have.

She picks *The Outlaw Josey Wales* because it's Mother's favorite and that will score her some points. After getting it ready to start, she goes to the kitchen to offer help.

Since Mother likes to pretend they're viewing a matinee at a real movie theater, she always prepares soda with lots of ice, a bowl of microwave popcorn, and a family-sized box of Milk Duds. They carry these to the TV room and when Nicki sits on the couch, Mother settles right beside her, too close as always. She wouldn't like it in any case, but the worst part is Mother's perfume that stinks like the stuff they spray on in summer to keep away the mosquitos. Mingled with the scent of popcorn and fake butter, it makes her food taste bitter. Despite this, she's going to force down everything in her bowl so Mother doesn't get angry and accuse her of being ungrateful.

When Mother finishes eating, she dozes with her head flopped back on the edge of the couch. This is Nicki's chance to sneak into her room, if she can get up without her noticing. Since their arms are still pressed together, she begins a painfully slow process of pulling away. Just at the moment when they're no longer touching, Mother shudders and seems like she's going to wake up, but then she just turns her head sideways and continues snoring lightly.

Nicki moves with practiced stealth as she lifts her weight off the couch and tiptoes out of the room. She hesitates, wondering if she should turn down the volume on the TV, but decides against it. Mother tends to notice any change to her usual settings.

Taking the stairs slowly, Nicki manages them without causing too many creaks. But just as her hand touches the door handle, Mother screeches from downstairs. "Nicki! Where are you?"

Her hope shrivels. "I'm just going to take a pee!" She hurries down the hall to the bathroom, shuts the door and uses the toilet. She'd been holding it in to use as an excuse anyway.

When she returns to the TV room, Mother has paused the film and is giving Nicki her squint eyes. That's how she looks when she's suspicious of something Nicki has done. "Why didn't you go down here?" she says.

"I don't like that toilet. You have to remember to hold the flusher down or it gets stuck."

This reminds Mother it irritates her too. "We need to get your uncle to fix that."

They watch the little bit remaining of the movie together, and then while the credits roll, Nicki gets up and carries the dishes into the kitchen to be washed. Uncle returns home while she's rinsing the glasses.

"You're out of your room?" he says.

Nicki is about to answer when Mother joins them from the hall. "We watched a movie. Nicki, go back upstairs now. I need to talk to your uncle."

"Yes, Mother." She places the second glass in the dish rack and restrains herself from skipping as she leaves the kitchen. Now is her chance, while the two carry on a private conversation they don't want Nicki to hear for some reason.

Still, she hesitates when she reaches the upstairs hall, thinking if she's caught, it will undo everything she's gained from her perfect behavior today. On the other hand, if she doesn't act now, she may not get another chance for a very long time.

The cadence of their voices wafts up the stairs. If she's lucky, the conversation will continue until Mother has to leave. She works nights at JJs Bar & Grill and according to Nicki's watch, that's in twenty minutes. But while her mind weighs the options, her body moves gingerly to Mother's door, pressing it open and slipping inside without a sound.

She's come with a specific purpose. Mother made the mistake of bringing her a collection of contemporary short stories, including one in which the protagonist has to pick a lock using two bobby pins. The author, a master of realism, included detailed instructions.

Mother often uses them to fasten her hair. At first, Nicki thought she would simply ask her if she could borrow some for the same purpose. But Mother has an untrusting person-ality that makes her suspect any change in behavior, no matter how insignificant. If she had any idea bobby pins could be used to pick locks, she would refuse Nicki's request and keep a careful eye on her supply from then on.

Nicki begins her search with the top drawer of the dresser, though she regrets this choice when it immediately scrapes against its frame. She nudges it closed again, resolving to save it as a last resort. It occurs to her the bathroom is a more likely place for anything to do with Mother's appearance.

It gets all quiet downstairs, giving Nicki a stab of panic, until Uncle says something again. His voice is always louder than his sister's.

She crosses the room, tiptoes into Mother's own private bathroom, and opens the left-hand drawer in the cabinet below the counter. It's crammed with cotton balls, old tooth-brushes, scissors, nail clippers, a pin cushion, and other random junk, but no bobby pins. She moves to the drawer on the right.

The conversation in the kitchen seems to waver again, but it might be that Mother is talking and can't be heard.

This second drawer is crowded like the other, but after reaching into the very back, Nicki draws out a clear plastic case filled with bobby pins.

A heavy step lands on the stairs. Uncle is coming.

Having gotten this far, she can't give up. She fumbles with the case but her hands are trembling and it flies out of her grip, landing on the floor with the bobby pins spilled out. She bites her lip to hold back a cry.

Mother must've said something to Uncle. His steps have paused and he's resumed talking.

Nicki gets down on her knees and gathers up the bobby pins, praying she hasn't missed any. She takes five or six and shoves them in her pocket. Closes the case and puts it back. Shuts the drawer.

The stairs groan under Uncle's weight as he continues up them.

Nicki runs, light-footed, to the door. There's no time to cross the hall to her own room; at this point, Uncle may see her from the stairs. Instead, she pushes Mother's door mostly closed, leaving it open just a crack as it was before.

Uncle arrives at the hall where he hesitates again.

Nicki shivers, poised behind Mother's door, listening to the click of the lock being turned on her room because he thinks she's in there. He moves on to his own bedroom and from the sound of it, goes in and shuts the door.

As soon as Nicki slips out, the tap of Mother's feet at the bottom of the stairs reaches her. There's nothing she can do but hope to god Mother doesn't hear her returning to her room. Once inside, she rushes to insert the bobby pins inside Cinderella's rump, setting down the bear only a second before Mother opens her door.

"I heard you come in the room." Mother's eyes squint with suspicion.

"I was in the bathroom." Let Uncle not be called for corroboration since he just walked past and must've seen it empty.

"Again? I didn't hear the toilet flush."

Nicki holds up her hands. "Not to pee. I washed my hands. They were still sticky from the popcorn." It's a terrible excuse since she was just doing dishes a few minutes ago, but nothing else came to mind.

Mother seems to have forgotten. "I have to go as soon as I

get changed." She approaches Nicki. "I appreciate your good behavior today." She gives her a squeeze. "Love you."

"Love you too," Nicki says. Once this was true, but now she's no longer sure what she feels for her. When Mother turns the lock again after going out, it's another notch in the coil of anger and resentment that has wrapped itself tightly around her heart.

Looking back at her textbook, she wonders if there's any point in doing the work. Mother isn't ever going to let her go to college. It's just another of her lies.

Rising, she goes to the window and gazes out at the shed. Even if through some miracle she finds a way to leave home someday with their permission, she can't make Sadie wait that long. Someone has to help her now, and there is no one but Nicki to do it.

She will practice with the bobby pins tonight.

Chapter Eight

IT WASN'T possible for Rebecca to prepare for the mind-blowing strangeness of reverting from an adult-sized body to that of a six-year-old. Gaping down at her skinny little self—mostly bare except for a bright yellow bikini—with her matchstick arms, stubby fingers, and short pudgy feet, she fights a powerful urge to flee. Running won't change a thing, nor will it calm her panicked, racing heart.

Water splashes her in the face and she realizes she's standing in the path of the sprinkler.

"Run!" Sadie shouts, herself in a purple flowered suit, waddling through and pausing when she gets beyond reach of the water.

Hardly aware of the soaking, Rebecca turns to the sister she hasn't seen for nineteen years. A mix of grief and joy overwhelm her, blurring her vision, tightening her chest. She wants to go to her, but the length of her stride falls short of her normal expectations, so that she pitches straight over onto her face.

"Becca, what are you doing?"

Becca. No one but Sadie ever called her that. Though her nose hurts, she jumps back up to her feet, aware of a feathery sensation of lightness. "Sadie, come here." Her childish voice sounds all wrong to her ears, high-pitched and lispy.

They meet outside the range of the sprinkler and Rebecca grabs her sister before she can escape, holding her tight. "Sadie… Sadie… Sadie… I missed you… I love you."

Sadie struggles in her grip and lets out a scream. "Mommy! Becca's hurting me!"

The backdoor slams and footsteps approach. "Rebecca, let go of her!" their mother calls out.

Only her presence could've pried Rebecca from her sister. She releases Sadie and watches as her long-deceased mother sweeps her long-missing sister up into her embrace. Her mother makes soothing noises as her gaze shifts to Rebecca and grows hard. "What did you do to her?"

Rebecca stands rooted, mouth open but no words coming out. Her body shakes like she's at the North Pole instead of sweltering-hot California in July.

Their mother lowers Sadie before approaching Rebecca. "What's going on?" Seeing how traumatized her oldest daughter appears, she softens her tone.

"Sorry, Mom," Rebecca squeaks.

"Are you sick?" Her mother glances at Sadie, worried she might catch it.

Rebecca shakes her head and closes her eyes, struggling to calm herself. Her mother pats her shoulder. "It's all right."

When she opens her eyes again, her mother is leaning over her and Rebecca realizes the few remaining photos of her don't do justice to the vitality of her living face. Moreover, until this moment, she hadn't grasped how similar they were. It's a bit like gazing into a mirror, with her mother only seven years older than Rebecca's age in real-time. Their hair is different but the structure of their faces, the shape of their eyebrows, and the lift of their lips on one side in irritation—these are the same.

Her mother is more beautiful though, with golden hair shining in the sunlight, framing her face in soft, natural curls. Her skin is lightly tanned, her eyes dusty green, nose straight, chin firm. She wears a sleeveless lilac blouse and slim jeans. Her gaze softens when it shifts to Sadie, radiating warmth. Her clear preference stabs like a needle through Rebecca's heart. Still, she can't resist clasping her mother's waist with her T-rex arms, the scent of her filling Rebecca with powerful feelings of remembrance and belonging. She isn't sure whether it's perfume or shampoo or something else, only that its smell is a familiar one, minty with the hint of cucumber.

"Sorry, Mom," she says in her childish voice. "Sorry for everything." The *everything* is loaded with meaning for her, meaning her mother doesn't yet understand.

"You're wet, honey." Her mother gives her a swift squeeze before pulling back. "Hey, you're not in trouble. There's nothing to be upset about. Let's go inside."

As they follow her into the house, Sadie approaches and takes Rebecca's hand. She then seems surprised when her big sister grips her back instead of batting her hand away. The real six-year-old Rebecca would have done that. But this Rebecca wishes beyond anything that she could find a way to hold onto Sadie forever.

The family room looks nothing like the one she visited yesterday. Her mother's workspace is positioned as Rebecca remembers it, next to the window where she can keep an eye on the girls playing out back. Her laptop open on the desk looks terribly dated but was probably state-of-the-art at the time. The rest of the furniture, from the plumpy couch to the notched wooden coffee table, is well-worn but comfortable. The stone fireplace that already has their initials carved into it gives Rebecca a feeling of reassurance. Several stains from spilled drinks mark the carpet, and the cream-colored walls sport a few pairs of child-sized fingerprints. Their parents' talk of fixing up the place is destined to come to nothing.

"Is Dad home?" Rebecca asks.

"What? You know he's at work," her mother says.

She does know he was at work this day, but she needs to confirm everything is as it was. Part of her deeply wishes he was here now, only so she could see him again too, before it all happened, and watch the way he interacts with Mom, Sadie, and her. Like with her mother, she isn't sure she can trust her memories of him.

"Get changed. I'll make you lunch," their mother says.

Sadie scampers up the stairs and into their shared bedroom, with Rebecca following at a slower pace, being cautious not to tangle her legs again.

Before returning here, she could not have described her childhood room other than to say it had twin beds. Seeing it now, everything comes back to her. The posters of dragons and unicorns. The coloring books and crayons on the desk she and Sadie shared. The matching midnight blue bedspreads with yellow stars and moons, covered with stuffed animals. She goes to the bookcase and looks at a *Magic Tree-house* novel. It strikes her funny to imagine her interest in time travel beginning with these books.

They take off their bathing suits and put on the clothes they left on their beds. Sadie wears a white tank with a purple unicorn on the front of it, and red shorts. Rebecca dons dark green stretch capris and a mint T-shirt decorated with butterflies.

"Come here, Sadie," Rebecca says, going up to the full-length mirror that hangs from their closet door.

Standing side by side, the girls look remarkably similar, partly because Rebecca is nearly as petite as her sister. Both have pale skin, button noses, and long hair in a nutty-brown shade. Rebecca wears hers loose over her back while Sadie's has been woven into two braids by their mother. Both have hazel eyes, but Sadie's still shine with a wide-eyed wonder that is gone from her sister's. They wear glitter polish on their finger- and toenails, gold for Rebecca and silver for Sadie. Rebecca always chose her color first and didn't allow her little sister to use the same.

Rebecca leans closer to the reflection and stares in awe at her face, so smooth and unblemished. She rubs her hand over her cheek, amazed by how soft it is.

"Lunch is ready!" their mother calls from downstairs.

A minute later the girls are seated at the kitchen table with glasses of milk and peanut butter and jelly sandwiches. Their mother was never creative when it came to meals, and Rebecca estimates they had PB & J at least fifty percent of the time. She hasn't had one in years, though, and finds herself looking forward to it, particularly since her stomach has been rumbling and now feels hollow.

After taking a few bites, Rebecca says, "How is your writing going, Mom?"

Her mother gives her an odd look. Probably it's the first time Rebecca has ever asked her that.

"Fine. Since when do you call me Mom?"

Rebecca is confused for a second before realizing she must've still called her Mommy at this age. In fact, there must never have been a time when she called her Mom. It was only while growing up and listening to her friends talk to their mothers that she started thinking of her as "Mom."

"Do you think you'll find a publisher for your book soon?" Rebecca says. She truly wants to know more about her mother as a working woman. She knows so little about her.

"Since when did you get interested in that?" She gives Rebecca a half-smile, bringing over their lunch. "I don't know. I hope so. My agent is working on it." While they start to eat, she gets out grapes and washes them.

Glancing over, she says, "Sadie, honey, you dripped jam on your pretty shirt!" She wets a paper towel and bends over her youngest daughter, wiping the spot. She kisses the top of her head.

"Why don't you love me as much as Sadie?" The words slip out of Rebecca. This is the only chance she'll ever get to ask her, but she should resist the temptation. If she does anything to change the trajectory of today, she might not get the answers she's looking for. If something she says or does makes her mother take them out instead of remaining home, for example, then she will have ruined everything.

Her mother freezes. "What did you say to me?"

She still has the power to terrify Rebecca. "Nothing."

"I treat you and your sister exactly the same."

"Uh huh." She feels as small as the body she now occupies.

"You've always wanted more attention," she says.

"Sorry, Mom. Mommy."

Sadie just keeps eating her sandwich, wisely staying out of the argument.

"Finish up now," her mother says.

Her appetite is gone. She can't eat the other half of the sandwich. "Can I eat it later?"

"After your nap, then."

Nap. Of course. It was required at that age.

The sisters rinse and dry their hands before running back upstairs to their bedroom. Sadie sits on the floor and begins dressing one of her dolls.

"What are you doing?" Rebecca says. "We need to nap." More accurately, she needs Sadie to nap so she can slip out of the room. If she does that while Sadie is awake, her sister will either try to follow her, or tell on her.

"I wanna play," Sadie says.

"I can't sleep if you do," Rebecca says. "You have to put your dolls away."

She ignores her.

"I'll tell Mom if you don't."

Sadie pouts but gets on her bed, bringing the doll with her.

"Close your eyes," Rebecca says.

Sadie closes them but they pop right back open. She clearly isn't sleepy enough.

Rebecca gets an idea and checks the bookshelf again. There it is, one of their favorites, *Where the Wild Things Are.* She pulls it out and sits beside Sadie on her bed.

"I'll read to you." She leans against the headboard while Sadie lies with her head in Rebecca's lap.

She reads the story slowly and in a soft voice to get Sadie to sleep, while gently smoothing the hair back from her forehead. It doesn't take long for her sister's eyes to close and breathing to thicken. Rebecca looks down at her angelic face, wanting to remember every aspect of it, wishing she could whisk her back to the present. How anyone could get it into their head to hurt such a creature, Rebecca will never understand.

Fortunately, Sadie is a deep sleeper even when just napping. Rebecca slips out from under her, opens her dresser and goes through her clothes till she finds jeans with deep pockets, and a pair of cotton socks. She changes into them before looking inside the closet for a pair of sturdy-looking shoes that will provide the best support. These go on quickly with Velcro closures.

Rebecca then checks the desk drawers for items that might be useful. It takes a minute to find a cheap plastic Aladdin watch that appears to be working. She keeps searching, looking for a flashlight but not finding one. She checks in the top drawer again, which is full of pencils and a few pens. That's when she spots it, a pen that's also a flashlight. She whisks it into her left pocket.

Pausing at the door, she presses her ear against it. Good news, Mom is talking on the phone and will be distracted from the noises Rebecca might make as she wanders about. She opens the door silently and creeps out into the hall. It's necessary for her to go downstairs, but since the lower section is in view of the family room, she gets on her stomach and slowly slithers down. When she reaches the bottom, she sneaks a peek toward her mother, happy to find her facing the other direction. From there Rebecca crawls on hands and knees to the kitchen, a much easier task at age six than twenty-five. Her limbs are so much more flexible than when she's an adult. Overall, she feels as light as the butterflies pictured on her shirt.

She stands when she reaches the kitchen. Somewhere there's a junk drawer that holds what she needs, if only she could remember which one. There are more drawers than she recalls, and each makes noise when she opens it. She starts with the outer ones, which seem a lot more likely to contain stuff that isn't useful for eating or cooking. The first holds waxed paper, aluminum foil, and plastic bags. The second has tape, pens, and notepads. When she pushes it closed, it moves too easily and bangs in the back.

This makes her cringe inside, especially after she realizes Mom isn't talking anymore. She may have hung up; she could be coming into the kitchen any minute now. This might be Rebecca's only chance. She whips open the third drawer, rattling its contents. It has tools, flashlights, matches… and the Swiss army knife. Snatching it up, she shoves it in her pocket, shutting the drawer with her other hand.

"What are you doing?" Mom says.

Rebecca whirls around to find her mother standing in the doorway. How much did she see?

"Looking for the tape," Rebecca says, afraid her childish face is not skilled at masking the lie.

Her mother approaches, narrowing her eyes. "What for?"

"Um… I… um… I drew a picture and wanted to tape it up on my wall."

"You know you're not supposed to do that."

She hangs her head. "I forgot. Sorry, Mommy." Hopefully she won't ask to see the picture.

"Your nap isn't over either. Go to your room. And stay there till I say you can come out."

"But Mom…"

"You heard me."

She knows this mood. There's no point in arguing. But just as she has resigned herself to returning upstairs, the sharp ring of the doorbell makes them jump.

"Oh who could that be?" Her mother is annoyed.

Knowing the answer, Rebecca follows her mother to the front door. Rebecca's friend Mikayla bounces on the doorstep, looking ready for a child photo shoot, with her wavy blond hair in a ponytail and her pink sunglasses shaped like hearts. She wears a crisp pink button blouse, a pink plaid skirt, and pink flip-flops. Her outfits are always coordinated because her mother works in fashion.

Mikayla's mom hovers behind her on the walkway in a designer sundress and white high-heeled shoes. "Camille, would you mind terribly watching her for a few hours?" she says to Rebecca's mother. "My father's just gone to the hospital and needs my help."

Her mother answers politely though Rebecca can tell she isn't pleased. "Oh no, what happened?"

"He's had a small stroke apparently."

"I'm sorry. Sure, Mikayla can stay here."

"Thanks a million. I owe you one." Mikayla's mom walks with swaying steps toward her car, being careful not to get her heels stuck in a crack.

Sadie runs down from her nap just as their mother is closing the front door. Rebecca's punishment forgotten, their mother says, "You can play in the backyard." This is her code for, *stay out of my hair while I work.*

As Sadie and Mikayla dash through the sliding door to the back of the house, Rebecca lingers. This is likely the last time she'll see her mother. At this moment, she wants nothing so much as to stay here by her side and grow up all over again. With the knowledge of foresight, she can make things different in this timeline. She can prevent Sadie from being taken. She can try to figure out how to win her mother's love. The years will pass as their family flourishes. She will not reach the age of twenty-five riddled with guilt and regret, alienated from the one parent she still has.

But it isn't possible. Before long, she'll be drawn back to her own time. There isn't anything she can do to prevent it.

Her mother has already returned to her computer. Rebecca runs to her side and reaches up to kiss her cheek. "I love you, Mommy," she tells her.

Her mother looks startled but not unhappy. "I love you too, Rebecca."

It will have to be enough. The phone rings and her mother turns away, settling into her chair and pressing the receiver to her ear like she expects this to be a long one. Rebecca knows it's a call from the literary agent.

When she emerges from the house, Mikayla hurries to her side. Exactly as she did in the past, Mikayla suggests in a whisper that they ditch Sadie during a game of hide & seek. That this suggestion came from her friend did little to assuage Rebecca's feelings of guilt over the years, probably because she had readily agreed. But now for the first time she wonders what effect this had on Mikayla. Their friendship ended after Sadie's disappearance. Was Mikayla also living a life full of fear and self-doubt? Did she need therapy to get through it? If Rebecca manages to survive this experience, she thinks she'll look her up in the present. Maybe it will help both of them heal. Most likely not, though.

Despite hating herself for it, Rebecca must go along with the plan. But first she wraps her arms around her sister's delicate frame, and kisses the side of her head. "I love you, Sadie," she whispers. When she backs away, both her sister and her friend are giving her odd looks.

"Sadie, we're playing hide and seek and you're it," Mikayla says.

Sensing there is no resisting her, Sadie merely nods before turning away to count.

"You have to hide your face at the tree," Mikayla commands.

Sadie casts her a long-suffering look, goes to the tree, and presses her hands and face against it. "One, two…" She knows how to count to twenty.

The two older girls run away and quietly sneak into the garage through the door at the side of the house. Her parents never park on one side so the kids can use it for hopscotch and other games. She tells Mikayla to draw the hopscotch board. "I have to go outside for a sec," she says.

"Don't let Sadie see you."

"I won't."

Since Sadie will come out to the front on the other side of the house, Rebecca waits next to the garage. She can't go to the yard yet, or the kidnapper might see her and drive away. But she stands on tiptoes to raise the latch and open the gate just a crack to allow her to watch for his arrival.

A minute later, Sadie dashes across the lawn from the other side and checks for Rebecca and Mikayla around the giant old oak tree. From her hiding place, Rebecca hears the noise of a car's engine, followed by its door opening. This has to be it. She slips through the gate to see.

The trunk of the car is raised. She glimpses Sadie inside it, pulling back her hand as the kidnapper slams the trunk closed. The engine is running and the driver's side door left open. He runs back to his seat, slamming the door shut and speeding away from their house.

The scene takes Rebecca's breath away. The horror of it. How fast it all happened. The thought of her baby sister frightened and alone.

But she has kept her head sufficiently to notice a few things. The car was a silver Ford Taurus with its license plate removed.

The kidnapper did not look anything like Bray Reamer.

Despite this, she sets off as fast as her miniature legs will take her down the street, and makes a right turn at the end of it. She has to stick with the plan, because this stranger could be working with Reamer, and might be bringing Sadie to his house this very minute.

Chapter Nine

ANNOYED WITH HERSELF, Rebecca has to stop to catch her breath before she's even halfway there. She doesn't have the stamina of her adult persona, particularly since her half-sized legs must take more than twice as many steps as normal. Plus the constant checking for cars approaching behind her slows down her pace even further. An adult, especially one who lives in the neighborhood and recognizes her, is likely to stop and see what this child is doing away from home all by herself. Or her mother, alerted by Mikayla, might come this way looking for her and Sadie.

The roads are thankfully not busy, but when a car eventually does come along, she has to throw herself behind some prickly bushes that scratch her legs. She huddles there until the car has driven past, breathing in deeply to slow her racing heart before launching into another mad dash. A minute later, a gardening truck heads toward her from the opposite direction. She decides against hiding, which might only attract more attention given that she's already in their field of vision. It's the right decision; the truck continues past her without the driver even glancing her way.

Before too long, she reaches Reamer's street and ducks onto it, slowing to a trot, since at this point, she'll be able to see if the silver Ford comes up or down the road. When she rounds the next corner, she gets a glimpse of his so-far empty driveway. However, it's possible the kidnapper's Taurus is already in the garage.

Approaching, she keeps her eyes on the windows, trying to make out if anyone is inside or not. Seeing no movement at all, she continues to the wooden gate next to the garage, hoping to look inside if it has a window in the back. She has to jump up to reach the latch, but she can't get it to lift. After trying several times, she figures it must be padlocked on the other side. It makes sense Reamer doesn't want anyone wandering into the backyard and discovering his marijuana plants. Or whatever else he's up to.

She looks back at the front of the house. On the far side near the corner, a window is partly open, probably to catch some air on this hot day. Looking down at herself, she realizes she's actually scrawny enough to fit through it, without even opening it further.

Her hands go clammy thinking about it, though. What if she encounters him in the house? She shakes her head, forcing herself to focus on the task at hand. Get inside, find Sadie or any other proof that Reamer has a connection to her kidnapping.

She ducks down as she crosses the front lawn, hoping she's too short to be seen from inside. No one appears at any of the windows. It seems that he's not home, which would be the best possible situation. If so, she can hide and wait for his return, possibly with Sadie and the other man.

When she reaches the window, she glances behind her in case any neighbors are watching. But no one is about. It's a weekday and they're probably all at work. Turning back, she peers into the house at a family room not too different from her own, except everything looks older and more frayed.

She has to pull herself up onto the ledge as the window is a little high for her. The first time she doesn't manage it, but on the second try, she jumps and the momentum helps her body to swing up. She hooks her leg over the sill and slides into the room backward, landing with a thud.

Freezing in place, she listens for the sound of anyone coming toward her. All is silent, though. She sniffs the room, wondering if there could be a skunk nearby, before remembering that's what weed smells like to her. She never did want to smoke the stuff, even as a teenager.

It shouldn't take long to search this one-story ranch house. Crossing the hall to the kitchen and eating area, she looks out toward the back where marijuana plants grow in the open. It's astonishing he didn't get busted a lot sooner.

She continues down the hall past a bathroom to the first bedroom. It looks empty from the doorway but she decides her search must be thorough. The kidnapper might've left Sadie bound and gagged, while he and Reamer drove off to fetch something. Rebecca checks behind the bed, under it, and in the closet. No Sadie.

"Well, well, well, what do we have here? Alice in Wonderland?"

Rebecca yelps at the sound of Reamer's voice. He managed to creep up on her and now his form blocks the door. It's definitely him, with that neck tattoo and the same hulking shape—though he looks much younger than when she last saw him.

He laughs at her. "Need help findin' anything?" His voice is drowsy and his eyes half-lidded like he just smoked weed.

Panic gets her legs moving and she tries to tunnel past him to the hall, but he effortlessly bars her way with one arm before grasping her around the waist and picking her up.

"Ow! You're hurting me!" She struggles to break free.

He carries her to a chair where he sets her down.

"Little Missy, think you can get away from me?"

"Let me go. I got lost. I'm sorry I came here."

He laughs again. "You got lost and climbed in through my window to find your way? I guess the breeze from my backyard been blowin' up your nose."

"It stinks," she says.

His face darkens. "Smells better'n you. Somebody set you up to this?"

She gets an idea. "My friend dared me. But we agreed if I wasn't back in five minutes, she would run home and get her mom to call the police."

"Your friend, eh?" He glances out the front window. "Who's she, the invisible girl? Don't see anyone out there."

"She's already gone to tell her mom."

"I'm the one should call the cops and report you for breakin' and enterin'. Will if you try somethin' crazy like this again. Lucky you picked my house. There's more guns than people in Windlake. Fingers on the trigger faster'n they can see you." He nods toward the front door. "Go on now."

"I can go?" Her voice gets even squeakier with surprise.

"If you don't, I'll just put you to work in the garden."

She jumps up and races away from him, gulping for breath at the sound of him following her. Maybe he's been playing with her and won't let her leave. But then he says, "Sure you know your way back home?"

"Of course I do." She flings open the door and rushes out.

Her thoughts whirl inside her head. She has found not one single indication of Reamer being involved in Sadie's disappearance. Not the Ford Taurus, not the actual kidnapper, not Sadie. If he were the mastermind who organized the plot, he wouldn't be sitting around smoking weed by himself right now. He wouldn't be laughing when little girls broke into his house, nor would he send them merrily on their way.

She has to accept that what she has believed ever since Reamer was first arrested simply isn't true. He had nothing to do with what happened to her sister.

She remembers from her reading about his trial, how his lawyer kept emphasizing his client had *sold* underage porn, but not *produced* it. Reamer had seemed quite remorseful, saying he'd been desperate for cash at the time. He swore he never looked at it, which no one believed. For the first time, she wonders if he was telling the truth. His actions were still inexcusable, but his behavior today showed he was not someone who had it in him to harm a small child.

For years she convinced herself of his guilt because he was all they had. Now she knows differently. It wasn't Reamer at all. It was the man who drove up to their house, snatched Sadie, and threw her into the trunk of his car. He's the one she needs to find.

Chapter Ten

IT'S MORNING, Rebecca is twenty-five again, and her stomach is growling. Minutes after leaving Reamer's place, she tumbled back to the present, because she had learned all she could from that particular time jump.

She treats herself to a large breakfast at her favorite brunch spot. Eggs and hash browns and biscuits and a fruit plate. She has to keep up her strength for the grim task ahead of her.

As soon as she returns home, she goes straight to her computer and writes a detailed account of everything she can recall from her mindcast. The color and make of the kidnapper's car, and that it had no license plate. The unknown man's size—medium height, slim—and his actions. A full description of what happened at Reamer's house, including their conversation. She no longer believes he was involved, but that assessment could change yet again once she gains more information.

Unfortunately, she was too far away to glimpse the kidnapper's face, partly covered by sunglasses and a black baseball cap. Along with these, he wore a plain black T-shirt and blue jeans. No team logos or anything else on the cap or shirt. She didn't manage to see his shoes, but no doubt they were as nondescript as the rest of his outfit.

When she's done, she opens a new window and searches on photos of "serial killers in California." Some are truly horrific, with wild eyes and fascist tattoos like Charles Manson—people you would guess are crazy just by looking at them. Then there are the others, the Ted Bundy types, who look normal, with pleasant or even handsome features. The guy they called the Dating Game Killer, because he was a contestant on that show, where young men or women interviewed prospective dates who were hidden from view, and chose one based on personality, not appearance. Amazingly, the Dating Game Killer was picked out of his group of three, but later, the woman refused to go out with him because she found him "creepy."

When Rebecca limits her search to those who were alive and not imprisoned in July, 2000, the list grows shorter. When she further reduces the field to those no older than forty at the time, few remain. She isn't certain about this, but from her brief glimpse, she thinks Sadie's kidnapper was young.

She expands the search to include convicted rapists and pedophiles, which greatly complicates her job. In many cases only the names are listed and she has to delve deeper to find photos. After six hours of this, she suffers from dry eyes and blurry vision, and the faces have all melded into one amorphous blob.

Her only real hope of identifying the kidnapper lies in a second mindcast. Her brain cries out against it and wants to delay indefinitely. Her heart, though, feels the urgent need to push forward and learn her sister's fate while she still has the ability to travel through time. For all she knows, it could end as suddenly and unexpectedly as it began.

Her heart wins the battle as nighttime approaches. She orders pizza to be delivered and opens a bottle of premium cabernet she has been saving for a special occasion. Unearthing a particularly challenging puzzle, she distracts her brain during her meal.

When she gets into bed, she makes her most effortless transition ever back to her childhood home, arriving at roughly the same time as before. This will allow her to gather the necessary tools again during naptime.

She repeats the actions of the day in listless fashion, determined not to dwell on whether this will be her last visit here to see Sadie and her mother. Her focus must be on setting up the right outcome. After Mikayla arrives, she takes off for the backyard with her and Sadie without looking back. Like before, she hears the phone ringing behind them in the house, and her mother picking up.

But this time, in answer to Mikayla's suggestion to ditch her sister, Rebecca says, "No, that isn't nice. Let's all play hopscotch in the garage." What she should've said nineteen years ago, in other words.

Mikayla likes to be in charge and therefore doesn't give up easily. "Oh, c'mon. You know Sadie's really bad at jumping."

Her twenty-five-year-old self is not about to defer to a six-year-old. "Sadie, let's play hopscotch," she says by way of answer to Mikayla.

Though her friend makes a face, she follows them into the garage, not wanting to be stuck alone in the backyard either.

Rebecca checks her watch, beginning to worry that time is running out. She knows the kidnapper will drive by soon.

"You draw the squares," Rebecca tells Mikayla, in her new role as the boss of them. She hands her a thick piece of chalk. "My mother made some chocolate chip cookies. I'll go see if they're ready."

Mikayla is about to argue, but the cookies shut her up. She loves sweets.

"I'll help you," Sadie tells Mikayla, luckily not mentioning anything about Mom not having made cookies at all.

Rebecca points at some coloring books. "No, you color. Let Mikayla do it." Her friend would balk at Sadie's help.

Her sister doesn't much like the new extra-bossy Rebecca either, but she still does as she says. Rebecca gives her a quick pat on the shoulders since there's no time for any more hugs, before hurrying out to the gate and lifting the latch on tiptoes. She dashes across the yard and around the oak tree to the sidewalk. The street is empty, of course. If anyone had been around, they could've witnessed what happened. The only people who might've seen anything were not home that day. The retired couple who lived across the street had gone to the reservoir to paddle their canoe.

She's not at all sure the kidnapper will take her. He could drive right past her, not interested. Although she and her sister bear a strong resemblance, he might realize she's older. Rebecca is more of a tomboy, especially now with her jeans and sneakers. Sadie is cuter and looks particularly girlish in the little red shorts she's wearing today.

At least the man might slow down enough for Rebecca to get a better look at him. But her goal is to get him to take her, no matter how terrifying the prospect. It's best for her to spend as little time as possible contemplating what she's doing —setting up her six-year-old self to be kidnapped. Her, a little kid with a Swiss army knife, a pen-flashlight, and an Aladdin watch.

A shudder grips her. She could die, and no one will ever know Sadie's kidnapper claimed a third life this day.

To give the impression she has come out here to play by herself, she finds a broken branch and uses it to bat a pebble around. Otherwise, the kidnapper might think she's waiting for an adult to arrive and pick her up.

Her leg muscles tighten as she hears an approaching car. She acts like she doesn't notice, but glimpses the vehicle out of the corner of her eye. A convertible. It continues past her.

When the pebble rolls into the street, she runs to fetch it. The sound of a second car makes her back away and look up. *The silver Ford Taurus.* It stops sharp at the curb, the trunk pops open, and the door flings out. The driver reaches her in several rapid strides. He grasps her around the waist and tosses her into the trunk like she's no heavier than a chicken. She wants to scream but bites down on her lip. She can't allow herself the chance of being rescued without having any idea who he is yet. Anyway, it all happens so fast, before she can even look at him, the trunk is banged down, his door slams shut, and the car bursts forward.

The plan has worked.

Chapter Eleven

WITHIN THE BELLY of the beast, Rebecca is bathed in perspiration, lying on some sort of filthy cotton comforter. Darkness blinds her while musty air that reeks of sweat and mold saturates her nostrils.

She knew he was going to put her in the trunk—she watched him do it to Sadie. But it's more harrowing than she could've imagined. Between claustrophobia, the threat of suffocation, and anxiety regarding the kidnapper's plans for her, she has an abundance of things to freak over. Her heartbeat races, and between this and the heat like the inside of an oven, she wonders if she'll survive the trip. Wonders if her sister survived it.

Struggling to hold down the panic, she takes long, slow, deep breaths. At least she can stretch her limbs. As an adult she would be all folded up and her muscles would be cramping.

As the car turns a corner, her body shifts and a plastic bottle rolls against her. She remembers her penlight and flashes it on. Seeing it's water, she opens the cap, glad to hear the click of a sealed bottle though she would've drunk it anyway. She slurps greedily but not too long because it needs to last. It may be a good sign, finding this here. It means he doesn't plan to kill her right away.

Rebecca sprays the light again, wondering if anything else is in the trunk. She nearly whoops for joy on finding a license plate. Finally, a stroke of luck. He must've removed it so it wouldn't be spotted while he drove through her neighborhood. Even better, it has a current California registration sticker, meaning the plate should be legit and traceable. She keeps the light on it while she memorizes the sequence.

Lying on her back, she repeats the number/letter combination over and over in her thoughts. She devises a memory game to help her recall it. No matter what else happens, she must return to the present with that license securely tucked inside her head.

Everything she's found so far indicates this kidnapping was planned. He took off the license plate. He put water and a blanket in the trunk. He removed possible weapons like the jack. He must've been waiting for just the right opportunity to snatch a lonely little girl up off the street.

Naturally, it didn't occur to him that leaving the plate in the trunk might be a bad idea. Few children would understand its significance. Although Sadie knew her numbers up to twenty and could recite the alphabet, she didn't have the presence of mind to memorize anything that wasn't repeated to her many times.

The kidnapper has the radio playing. It sounds like some kind of political commentary, though she can't clearly make out what's being said. Every now and then he responds to it, arguing with the guy on the radio. *Well, how stable could someone be who goes around snatching little girls?*

She isn't sure how much time has passed when the car slows down and gradually comes to a stop. Her small body trembles. If he opens the trunk, it's going to be hard to resist making a run for it if she gets the chance, but she can't leave without learning more about him. The license plate could be stolen from another vehicle and might not be any help at all. She needs to find out his name, or the address of their destination. Preferably both.

The car door creaks as it opens. Footsteps crunch on gravel. There's a beep, and the trunk pops open. She squints at the bright sun behind his dark silhouette but doesn't squirm, wanting to show him she's going to be cooperative. For now.

"You doing okay?" His words come out like he's striving carefully to form them.

She pulls herself into a sitting position, hoping he won't object, and gets her first real look at his face without the sunglasses, which he must've left in the car. On the left side, his eyelid and mouth droop unnaturally, like he has some kind of paralysis. There's a bit of drool at the bottom of his lip on that side. Reacting to her scrutiny, he takes out a cloth handkerchief and wipes it.

Her first instinct is to pity him. If he had this appearance as a child, he would've been ruthlessly bullied. But her heart hardens again almost instantly. *He took Sadie and did who-knows-what to her.* No mercy. No forgiveness.

Her thin, childish voice says, "It's very hot in here."

"Yeah, sorry about that." His "s" is slurred a bit, like a cross between "sorry" and "thorry." He talks slowly, enunciating each word. She thinks the paralysis may have forced him to adopt a more deliberate manner of speaking.

He glances at the water bottle. "You found it. Good." He

reaches into a backpack at his feet and puts another bottle in the trunk, along with a bag of generic hard candy.

"Thank you," she says.

He musses her hair in what is meant to be a friendly gesture, making her flinch. "You're a polite little girl, aren't you?"

"I want to go home." She says that mainly because he will expect it.

"We'll be there soon."

This answer surprises her. But he is probably referring to *his* home. Or to wherever he is going to bring her.

"Can I ride in the backseat? I'll be quiet."

"You seem like a good kid. But you have to stay here. Sorry." He reaches past her for the license plate, then kneels and takes a screwdriver from the backpack. Rebecca looks past him at trees, a dirt road. It appears he pulled off the freeway to this deserted location. He starts screwing the license plate back on.

"But it's so hot, I might die."

He pauses. "I don't think so. Anyway, you can't sit up front so I don't want to hear any more about it."

Not wanting to annoy him, she waits a moment before speaking again. "Where are we going?" She needs to get as much information as she can, in case her trip is cut short.

"You'll see."

"Is it in the mountains?"

"I said, you'll see."

"What's your name, mister?"

"Call me Uncle." He continues with the second screw.

"Uncle who?" Fishing for a name.

"Just Uncle."

Creepy Uncle No-Name. She decides she's not going to call

him anything, while dubbing him *Bob* as in the expression *Bob's-your-uncle*, inside her head. "My name is Rebecca Danser," she says, still fishing.

"Is it?" He makes a face like he smells something bad. She'd like to tell him if he wants to experience a truly terrible stench, he should get inside the trunk.

"Well, Rebecca, I expect you to do everything I tell you," he says. "If so, you'll get more candy and other good things."

Like I want your fucking Walmart candy. "What if I don't?" she says because she wants to know what kind of threats he's going to use against her.

"If you disobey me, I'll shut you in a dark room all by yourself. If you try to run away, I'll find you wherever you are and I might have to hurt you."

Fury fills her as she pictures actual four-year-old Sadie sitting here being terrified by him. If she were an adult with a gun, she would probably shoot him right now.

She forces herself not to think about her sister and instead concentrate on the details of his appearance. Of course, the facial paralysis is enough to recognize him if she learns where to look for him in the present. But other details could still be helpful and might give additional clues regarding his identity. He has blond hair in a short cut he might've done himself, a scar just above his right eyebrow, blue eyes, and a ski-jump nose. His eye teeth protrude like someone who never wore braces. And he wears a silver chain around his neck, with a round silver pendant that has the silhouette of a Labrador or similar type of dog etched inside it. Maybe he wears this all the time, or maybe just today. She would put his age at early twenties. He's medium height, thin, even scrawny.

The man has no visible tattoos or piercings, which makes

her wonder if he had a strict upbringing in a conservative family, with a father who might beat the crap out of him if he ever did anything to express himself. The neat way he's dressed supports this idea. His T-shirt is tucked into his belted pants, which look like they might've been ironed. He wears clean leather work boots.

His hands reveal a couple of chipped nails, and some dark staining near the fingertips. Like he works in a dirty profession. Factory worker? Farmhand? Chimney sweep?

He finishes with the license plate and stands up. "You need to pee?"

"When will we get to where we're going?" she says, continuing to push for more information.

"You need to pee or don't you?"

She nods, not knowing when she'll get another chance. Before she can crawl out, he takes her under the arms and lifts her from the trunk, filling her with revulsion. He points out a tree close to the car. "You can go behind there. Don't try to run away. I told you what would happen."

"I won't. Do you have toilet paper?"

He scowls. "Just go."

She hurries behind the tree, lowers her pants and squats. It occurs to her, what if this is the exact place her sister went to relieve herself after she was taken? It makes her want to reach out and touch the tree. *Sadie, I'm with you.*

Without paper, she shakes her bottom before lifting her pants. She wishes she could go anywhere but back to that man, back inside the trunk of his car. But she has to follow this through. She has to find out where he's taking her.

When she returns, he lifts her into the trunk and shuts it over her.

Chapter Twelve

REBECCA HAD CHECKED her watch when kidnapper Bob stopped the car to put the plate back on. Forty-five minutes had passed since he grabbed her from in front of her house. Ten more minutes elapsed before he resumed driving.

Another fifteen minutes go by before she feels butterflies in her stomach from the up and down motion of a hilly road. Soon they're weaving more frequently from side to side as well, giving her the full rollercoaster experience. These are the indications that they've come to the Sierra Foothills and are headed into the mountains.

She can tell they're no longer on a freeway, because they've paused several times at what feel like stop signs. Fifty more minutes pass before they come to what must be a traffic light. Then two more lights before their speed increases like they're back on the highway. In eleven minutes, she hears the tick-tick-tick of the turn signal and feels the Taurus cut to the right. They slow significantly and follow a windy road until coming to a stop eight minutes later.

Is this their destination? She checks her watch again to

confirm it's been roughly two hours total—information she tucks away along with the license plate number.

She hears him get out and a second later the trunk opens. Her eyes accustomed to darkness have to squint up at Bob, who's framed by a mantel of trees behind him. "Is this it?"

"Yeah. You keep quiet now."

She stumbles on weakened knees when he sets her down next to the car, and he has to pull her back up again. Ignoring him, she scans the property for any useful details. It's an isolated, heavily treed lot with a partly crumbling paved driveway. They've arrived in front of an unattached single-car garage, the size of a windowless cabin. On the other side of the driveway, pulled off to the side, a small, old-fashioned pickup truck is parked facing them. Rebecca would love to get its license number too, but to her extreme disappointment, it has no plate in the front.

A rust-brown two-story house with wood siding and a steeply sloped shake roof looms across the short walkway. Once it may have been charmingly rustic, but now it looks dilapidated, in need of fresh paint and repairs. The windows are dark, and try as she might, she can't see anyone through the glass. Most likely he lives alone in a house inherited from his parents, who must've abused him to turn him into the monster he is.

"This way." He grabs her hand with his sweaty palm causing her insides to clench up, and leads her around the side of the house to a clearing in the back covered in leaves and pine needles. She glimpses what could be a stagnant pond on one side. On the other, raised up on a small hill, squats a building that's big for a shed, but small for a cabin.

"Where are we going?" She tries to wrench her hand out of his grip, panic welling up inside her.

"Stop it." He drags her to the building and holds her with one hand while the other gets a key from his pocket and unlocks the door. When they're both inside, he shuts the door behind them and lets go of her.

The inside looks hastily prepared, with a twin mattress on the floor made up with sheets, blankets, and a flat pillow. A child-sized table and chair are propped against the wall. Toys and a few worn stuffed animals with matted fur are piled in a box. A bucket covered by a piece of wood sits in the corner, with toilet paper beside it. *Thanks for your consideration, asshole.*

There's barely enough floor space for them to stand without stepping on the bed. One small window, too high for little-girl Rebecca to reach, provides scant light. She glances around the small area for lamps without seeing any. "Can you turn on the light?" she asks to check this.

"There's no electricity." He moves to go.

"You can't leave me here!" This is real, he's planning to lock her inside, and the thought of being his prisoner, and what he might do when he returns, fills her with dread. Whatever her mind may be, her body is six-years-old and she's completely at his mercy.

"Calm down. I don't want to hear a word out of you." He pauses at the door and perhaps in response to the expression of sheer terror on her face, he says, "I'll be back," as if that could be comforting to her instead of only making things a thousand times worse.

His footsteps recede toward the house and as soon as she hears a door bang shut, she takes out her Swiss army knife. If she has any hope of escaping, it needs to be while she still has light to see inside the shed. But there's no keyhole on the inside for her to use to pick the lock, if she were even capable of doing that. Fighting off a feeling of desperation, she tries to insert her knife between the door and its frame, but the fit is too tight. Throwing down the knife in frustration, she hurls herself against the outward opening door, but it's much too sturdy to be affected by her featherlight body and she only ends up hurting her shoulder.

If she could just get out, she could run down the driveway and possibly get the address from a mailbox, or the name of the street from a sign. This might make the difference between finding him in the present or not, especially if it turns out the license plate belongs to a stolen vehicle.

The window is the only way and she has only one chance of reaching it. She shoves the mattress to the side to make space on the floor before dragging the table to the area below the window, right up next to the wall. The chair is light, allowing even her weak and spindly arms to lift it and place it on the table. She folds her knife and pockets it before beginning the climb from floor to table to chair. Raising herself to a standing position, she steadies herself against the wall while the chair wobbles beneath her feet.

Rebecca reaches the latch and snaps it open. Lifting onto her tiptoes, she pushes the bottom of the glass outward as far as it will go. But she isn't sure whether she can squeeze through the narrow gap she's created.

"Hey!" The man shouts from the house.

Fuck. He must've seen the window come open, and now he's running to the shed. In seconds he'll have the door unlocked and who knows what he'll do to her then.

In her panic to get back down quickly and be ready to jab him with her knife, she loses her balance. The chair slips out from under her feet and she tumbles downward. The sound of the key turning in the lock reaches her at the same instant her head cracks against the floor.

Part III

Chapter Thirteen

NICKI HUNCHES over the game table staring down at the jigsaw. She and Uncle have been working on it for several days because it's hard. One thousand pieces. Uncle snaps one into a spot she'd given up on. They're nearing the end.

As usual, it's a picture of dogs doing doggie things. This one has a Doberman, a Golden Retriever, and a French bulldog being walked by owners who look like them.

She glances across the table at Uncle with the silver dog medallion dangling from his neck. "If you like dogs so much, why don't you ever get one?"

He answers without looking up. "You know Mother's allergic."

"Are you sure about that?"

He raises one eyebrow. The other doesn't move because of his paralysis on that side. "She wouldn't lie about it."

"Yeah, but maybe she's mistaken. Maybe she happened to sneeze around a dog one time, but it wasn't the dog that caused it. There might have been chrysanthemums or some other flowers on a table nearby. Maybe that's what she's allergic to."

He presses another piece in place.

"You could test it, you know. Get some dog hair, I'm sure it's easy enough to find. Spread strands of it around the house. See what happens."

"That's crazy. She would get so angry if she found out." He dabs his lip with his handkerchief.

There was a time when she would've dearly loved having a dog at the house. But not anymore. Not if things work out the way she hopes. So she's not really sure why she even started this conversation, except that it annoys her how he constantly defers to Mother. His sister is eleven years older than him, and he's used to her telling him what to do ever since he was a baby. But it could be he never challenges her because she's clever enough to let him have his way in the stuff that's important to him.

Footsteps tap down the stairs and Mother appears, ready for work. She always wears a button blouse with a bow that ties at the collar, a straight skirt, nylons, and shoes with sensible heels.

"It's so nice to see the two of you playing together," she says like they're eight-year-old siblings. She bends to kiss Uncle on the side of his head. "Why don't you eat the fish sticks and tater tots tonight? There's carrots to go with it in the fridge." She always has carrots with her fish because she likes dipping them in the tartar sauce.

"Okay," Uncle says.

She comes around the table and pats Nicki on the shoulders. "You be good now."

Nicki ignores her, pretending to concentrate on searching for a piece.

Mother hates not getting a response. "Aren't you going to wish me a nice night at work?"

"Have a good night," Uncle says.

Nicki still doesn't respond and Mother turns away in a huff. "If someone hopes to get back full privileges, someone ought to start being nicer around here." She goes out the door and a minute later, the car starts up.

"She just wants what's best for you," Uncle says.

"Does she?" They've been saying these sorts of things for years, but Nicki no longer believes them.

"Course she does." He wipes his mouth.

"You can finish the jigsaw." Nicki rises. "I've got school work to do." She goes upstairs to her room and works on geometry until Uncle calls her for dinner.

Unsurprisingly, he's prepared the menu ordered by Mother. Nicki neither loves nor hates the meal; she's pretty neutral about everything she eats. It provides nourishment but not pleasure.

"How come we never get to eat hot dogs?" Nicki says, still feeling ornery.

Uncle frowns. "You know Mother doesn't like them."

"Yeah, but how come you and I can't have them?" Somewhere deep inside her memory, she remembers eating a hot dog smothered in ketchup and loving it.

"We all eat the same meal. Mother says it's a lot more work to make something different for everybody."

"Seems to me it's pretty easy to cook a hot dog."

"How would you know?"

Nicki doesn't answer, annoyed with this reminder that she doesn't get to know how to do anything they don't want her to learn. After a minute, she asks, "Do you ever get tired of doing what Mother says all the time?"

"She's good to me. She mostly lets me do what I want." He doesn't get how strange this sounds coming from an adult.

"If you're nice to her, she'll be good to you too," he adds.

"I'll try harder," she says, not really meaning it. "Can I bring Sadie her food tonight?"

Uncle stiffens up and wipes his lips with the napkin. "I already did."

She's not sure she believes him. "Can I just visit with her then? She must be so lonely."

"Not tonight. Mother says you have to earn back your privileges."

"Oh Mother this, Mother that!" She flings down her fork. "Screw that."

"Watch your language. And finish your meal." His voice has turned cold and harsh.

She lowers her head and picks up her fork. "Yes, Uncle."

Later when she's doing the dishes, he interrupts her. "Going out to chop some wood."

She glances toward the window. It's still early in the evening and the summer sun hasn't yet set. She resists the temptation to reply with sarcasm. *Don't we have a ten-year supply already?* He is out there chopping year-round. When she questioned him once before, he'd said, "Someone has to do it. We live in a forest. Can't just let logs rot on the ground."

"I need you to go to your room," he says.

"But you'll be right outside."

"Mother said that's the rule for now. One of us has to be inside if you're to have the run of the place."

Without arguing further, she turns off the water, dries her hands, and goes up the stairs with Uncle right behind her. After she shuts her door, she hears him lock it.

A zip of excitement runs through her. This is the first

chance she's gotten to try out the bobby pins. Checking the window, she waits to see him come out back carrying his axe to the woodpile. Then she takes out the bobby pins and gets to work on the door. *Thwack, thwack* forms the background noise as she uses a bent pin as a lever to keep tension on the lock while she picks it using a second pin.

She works slowly, trying to get a feel for it, listening for clicks as a sign of progress. Fifteen minutes later, she still hasn't opened it and her knees hurt, pressed against the bare wooden floor by the door. After grabbing her pillow to put under them, she restarts from the beginning.

Ten more minutes pass without success and she pauses to rest her fingers. Outside, the *thwacks* have also stopped. *Crap.* She's about to put away her tools when the sounds of chopping resume. She dives back into her work, starting to feel as if she's getting the hang of it. Before long, the last pin clicks inside the lock and she turns the lever to open it.

Though it's the skill of a thief, her accomplishment fills her with pride. While Uncle continues with the wood, she locks and unlocks the door three times, getting faster with each attempt. She has confidence she can do it quickly now, but she'll continue to practice whenever she has the opportunity.

A glance at the window tells her the sun is nearly gone, and he'll be coming back inside soon. She locks herself back into her room, replaces the precious bobby pins, and goes to peer out the window at Uncle.

He puts the last log on the newest stack, wipes his hands with a towel, and pats his face with his handkerchief before heading across the clearing toward the shed. Pausing outside its door, he turns back toward the house, his gaze shifting to Nicki's window.

She jerks back behind the wall, but she might've been too late to prevent him from seeing her. Moving away, she rubs her hands against her jeans. Feeling dirty. Witnessing him there makes her feel like a party to his crimes. *Why haven't I helped Sadie yet?* Nicki bears responsibility as long as she allows herself to be paralyzed by fear of Mother and Uncle. It's not just about her. She can tolerate her life here with them. But she can't tolerate what they're doing to that little girl.

Getting an idea, she brings her pencil and writing pad to the bed and begins a list of everything they need to take with them when she and Sadie make their escape. At the top, she writes *Uncle's backpack*. She's seen him use it from time to time when he said he was going for a long walk. It should be just the right size for their needs, without weighing her down too much. The second item on the list is *map of the area*. There's one inside the kitchen drawer. When she gets an opportunity, she'll study it closely.

She doesn't know when the chance will come to make her move. But when it happens, she'll be ready. For Sadie.

Chapter Fourteen

REBECCA WAKES WITH A SPASM, vividly recalling how much it hurt to bang her skull against the hard surface of the cabin floor. Touching her head where the impact occurred, she no longer feels any pain or swelling, because that was six-year-old Rebecca and the mindcast has ended. She gazes at her adult-sized hand with affection, filled with relief to be herself again.

Sunlight floods her bedroom. Thirteen hours have gone by since she flipped into the past. She can't remember when she's ever remained in bed so long. Maybe her body needed extra time to recover from the trauma of the mindcast, disturbing beyond anything she's experienced in her life.

There are things she must do, but she can't get herself to move just yet. She's suffused with conflicting emotions of the sort she hasn't allowed herself to feel for years. Love, remorse, and longing for the living presence of her lost sister and mother. Judgment, guilt, and self-hatred regarding her actions that day, the worst of her life. Revulsion and loathing toward the man who destroyed her family. A man who now has a face, if not an identity.

Exultation underlies all of it. She's seen the man, and the license plate of the car he drove, and the place where he brought Sadie. So many clues, surely they'll lead her to him. She punches the pillow. It's impossible for her to fail now. She'll find him and bring him to justice, no matter how long it takes. No matter what she has to do. Determination surges through her.

Though her stomach craves food, she rises and goes straight to her computer. Opening a new document, she enters every detail she can recall. First the license plate number. Then a complete description of the kidnapper from head to toe. She even makes a sketch of his face. Unfortunately, she's incapable of drawing anything. Even her stick figures lack symmetry. Once when she played Pictionary, her partner couldn't guess a single one of her clues. No matter. Bob the Kidnapper suffering from facial paralysis greatly limits the field of possible suspects.

She records the details of their trip. The time it took for each section of the drive. The appearance of the clearing where they stopped, along with their conversation and all else that took place there. The sensations of riding in the car, the zigzags and ups and downs. The frequency of stop signs and stop lights. The times where traffic seemed to slow. And the final right turn off the highway.

Coming to her arrival, she describes the house and grounds. The clearing in the back, the possible stagnant pond, and the trees surrounding everything. *The shed.* She tries drawing a picture again, and although it's better than the face she sketched, it doesn't match her memory well enough. She crumples the paper and tosses it.

By the time she runs out of things to write down, she's tingling with anticipation. This has to be enough to find him, arrest him, and keep him from hurting any other little girls as he has hurt Sadie. She saves the document to her USB stick and prints out several copies. She will not be taking the chance of losing these notes, full of details that are fresh in her mind but will probably fade shortly.

She decides to place a copy of the document inside her letter to her father, telling him he can rely on the information though she can't tell him how she came by it. Most likely he'll consider it the ravings of a lunatic. But she will have tried.

Anyway, she's not planning on dying yet.

She wishes she could go to Freddie—the detective on Sadie's case with whom she still keeps in touch—and show him her description of Bob. Ask him to get a police artist to produce a sketch. Then have the police search their database for a match. But how could she possibly explain this description of the kidnapper that came out of nowhere? Everyone knows she never saw him, not even a glimpse from behind, because she was in the garage with Mikayla. She can't change that fact now, nineteen years later. Nor can she reveal her time-travel ability. Freddie isn't the sort to believe anything that doesn't sound rational. And even if she managed to convince him, what then? He'd be laughed off the force if he shared her story with any of the other officers.

Having completed her most pressing work, she allows herself to go out for another large brunch. She's been eating like a whale lately, just opening her mouth and letting gobs of food flow in. But a quick check on the scale shows no real change. The mindcasts seem to rob her of a great deal of energy that needs replacement in calories. She orders a stack of banana pancakes, planning to bring the leftovers home, but before she knows it, she has scarfed up the last bite soaked in maple syrup.

After leaving the restaurant, she sets out for a long walk since this version of her hasn't exercised in a couple of days. She calls Freddie, who doesn't answer—he never does—and leaves an urgent message for him to call back as soon as he can.

The phone rings half an hour into her walk and shows *Detective Lazo* on her display. "Hey Freddie, thanks for getting back to me so quickly."

"What's up? It's been a while." His voice still has the ability to comfort her.

"I've got new information. Can we meet somewhere in the next few days?"

There's a brief silence, and then, "You're in luck. I have to be in Milpitas this afternoon. Meet me at Kristal's Coffee on Hawthorne? Three p.m.?"

"Perfect."

They hang up without any more chatting. Freddie isn't the chatting type. Straight to business. Direct. Honest.

Rebecca returns home to shower and change. She reviews her notes, not planning to bring them with her to the meeting. Except she does jot down the license plate number on a slip of paper. If it connects to someone who lives within two hours of Windlake, she will be well on her way to breaking this case.

At the appointed time, she walks into the coffee shop to find Freddie already seated. He's a man of Chinese heritage on one side, Hispanic on the other. Trim and fastidiously dressed as always, he wears a sports jacket over a turtleneck, even though it's summer. Polished leather shoes. He rises when he sees her and shakes her hand when she reaches him.

He isn't the hugging type. As usual, he smells like soap and looks as if he shaved an hour ago. His short black hair is neatly gelled to his head.

He smiles, which for him involves only a slight broadening of the lips. "Good to see you, Rebecca."

"Thanks, you too." She sits across from him and they delay talking until they can both order coffee. Freddie gets a chocolate croissant to go with his. "Missed lunch today," he says. The man has a definite sweet tooth, though considering she just polished off enough pancakes to feed a youth soccer team, she's hardly one to talk.

"It's about Sadie's case. Of course." It isn't as though they meet for coffee any other time. She slides across the piece of paper where she's written the license plate number. "Can you find out who owned this car in the year 2000?"

Freddie's eyes widen in disbelief. "Are you saying this has something to do with the kidnapping?"

"Maybe. I can't be sure."

"Where did you get it?"

"An anonymous tip."

"Did this person call you?"

"Freddie, I'm sorry, but I can't say any more about it."

"If they called, I can trace the number for you," he says.

"They didn't call."

"Email then? It'll be harder to trace if they know what they're doing."

"No email."

"That leaves handwritten letter. Can I see it?"

"I didn't get a handwritten letter." So far, at least, she has stuck with the truth. "That's all I can say. Can you just trace the number? What harm is there in that?"

He taps his fingers on the paper before raising his gaze to

her. "I have to say this. If you found this source on the Internet… you can't trust information you find on the Internet. Nothing short of an article from a reliable source like the Times or the Post. Even then, it might've been doctored. Thousands of websites spout conspiracy theories. In some cases, people are trying to get revenge. What if whoever posted this has it in for whoever owns this vehicle? An ex-wife or ex-business partner. You can't believe stuff like this."

"It isn't like that," she says. "I swear."

"It's easy enough to find out all about the case. They could've targeted you. You didn't pay them, did you?"

"No." She knew it was going to be hard convincing him, but this is even worse than she expected.

He takes a bite of his croissant and chews thoughtfully. After a minute, he says, "I'll run it through and get the name of the vehicle owner. I suppose it can't hurt to do a quick check on them. See if they've got a record. If there's anything the slightest bit related, like he beat up his girlfriend or any other kind of assault, even if it's minor, it might be enough to justify talking to him. That's the most I can promise. But if the car owner is clean, never been busted for anything, I can't investigate. The chief would never approve it. I can't contact the FBI over this either. They'll think I'm crazy."

That he's agreed to run the plate fills her with joy. "Thank you, Freddie. That's all I'm asking." She had never imagined he would do more than this. Her fear had been that he wouldn't do anything.

He drains his cup. "Don't thank me yet."

Chapter Fifteen

FREDDIE'S CALL comes a few days later in the morning. "It's a silver Ford Taurus belonging to a Daniel Ortiz of Draywood. D-R-A-Y-wood. You know where it is?"

"I don't think so." She's opening Google Maps, typing the name of the town. When she sees the location, she pumps her fists, mouthing *yes*. "I see it. Part way up the mountains."

"That's right. A one-horse town. Population around two thousand."

She clicks on *Directions* and enters "Windlake." When the app displays a roughly two-hour drive between Draywood and her former hometown, she bites her lip to hold back a shout. *This is it.*

"Sorry to have to tell you this, but Daniel Ortiz has led an exemplary life. Sixty-eight years old. A retired carpenter. Well-respected member of his community. He donates to charities and never got worse than a speeding ticket. The man's a mensch."

Disappointment fills her, though she isn't too surprised. A criminal is a law-abiding person until they're caught.

"Does he still live there?"

"No, he moved to Lodi a few years back." His voice dips to a lower register as he takes on a sterner tone. "I want to caution you not to approach him. I don't know where you got this number, or what role you think the driver of that car played, but it's just wrong. You need to let this go. If you take matters into your own hands, I won't be able to protect you."

"I'm not going to do anything," she lies. He can truthfully attest to having no knowledge of her plans, if it comes to that. This will all be on her.

He hesitates like he's not sure if he believes her but can't decide if he should say so. "Okay then," he finally replies. "You take care."

"I will, Freddie. I appreciate your help, even if it didn't come to anything."

As soon as she hangs up, she goes to her computer and looks up Daniel Ortiz of Draywood. There isn't much about him, except confirmation he used to be a carpenter and active member of the Sierra Club. However, another Ortiz comes up. His son, Martin, who works as a real estate agent in the area.

She can't find a photo of Daniel online. In any case, he's too old to be the man who picked Rebecca off the sidewalk and brought her to the shed. Nineteen years ago, Daniel was forty-nine, but Bob the Kidnapper could not have been older than his mid-twenties.

His son Martin, though. Could he have been driving Dad's car? She looks him up next, and thanks to his being a real estate agent, there are plenty of photos online. Movie-star handsome, he's clearly not Bob with the facial paralysis, even if the condition had been cured somehow. Martin appears to be in his mid-thirties now, making him sixteen or seventeen when it happened. Maybe he was working with Bob. Or maybe the father had been working with him. For all she knows, they could all be part of a network of child traffickers located in the Sierras.

She drums her fingers on the desk, considering whether she should pay a visit on Daniel Ortiz in Lodi. But what good would it do? He isn't about to admit anything to her, and she'll just be alerting him to the fact that she's coming for him.

Looking back at the map, she checks the route. It's easy to spot an extended section of the highway where the road follows frequent twists and turns. Figuring how long it would take to reach there from her old house, she matches this roughly with her description of when the constant swerving inside Bob's car began.

Certainty grips her. Draywood is where he brought her. The route matches her sensations of the trip, and the Taurus was registered to a man who lived there. Draywood is where she must go.

A bit more research reveals that Martin now owns the house that used to belong to his father. This could even be where she was taken. With growing excitement, she looks at the satellite view of his address, but she can't get an image of the back, and too many trees block the front to allow her a clear view of the place. She has to go see it in person. Her first step will be to visit the house. Her second will be to look for Bob. In a town that small, how many people could there be with a face like his?

She knows if she delays leaving it will cause her to hesitate. Being captured by that demon has left her frightened to face him again. Though she's back to being twenty-five years old, she is smaller and weaker than most men. And for all she knows, Bob might have a stockpile of automatic weapons as well. She has nothing aside from a can of mace she's been keeping in a drawer. The thought reminds her to move it into her purse, and then to add a roll of duct tape to her pile of things to be packed. If she can disable him with the mace, she might have a chance to bind him to a chair or something.

Returning to her computer, she looks up information about the area. The town is tiny, with a highway running through it and businesses lined up on both sides of it. A few small restaurants and cafés, a grocery market, a burger joint and pizza place, several gas stations—probably to accommodate all the skiers headed up and down the mountain—some retail shops, two real estate offices, and one motel. The Draywood Motel has a website displaying photos of the lobby and the front of the building, a phone number, and an email address. With no online reservation system, it seems like a holdover from the 1990s. On closer observation, the place looks more *rundown* than *rustic*—their word—but still several levels above the Bates Motel. She briefly considers staying in a different town, but decides she would be better off close to the heart of things, as she tries to sniff out Bob from wherever he might be hiding.

When she calls to book a room, they sound surprised she bothered to make a reservation instead of just popping in while passing in the area. And when she asks if she can keep the number of days open, they have no objection whatsoever. She hopes she isn't the only guest in the whole place.

Her next call takes a little more preparation. She usually doesn't drink wine this early in the day, but she needs a few slow sips to calm herself. The man she's about to speak with might be a villain who was involved in her sister's kidnapping.

She practices what she'll say to him a few times before

finally making the call. After two rings, real estate agent Martin Ortiz answers, identifying himself in a clear, resonant tone. He probably spent years developing that voice, she thinks. It would go a long way toward convincing reluctant buyers to part with the obscene amount of money it takes to buy a home in California.

"Hi, this is Rebecca Jones," she says, having decided in advance to use a fake last name. If she were a real estate agent, she would Google every prospective client, and she expects no less of him. Particularly if in addition to selling real estate, he is somehow involved in child abduction. A search of *Rebecca Danser* shows her connection to missing child *Sadie Danser* on the first page.

Jones is a common enough name, he'll become overwhelmed trying to figure out which one might be her. She keeps her first name intact, knowing she'd be sure to forget to respond if she dubbed herself something else. "What do you think of that, *Susie?*" he might say, causing her to look over her shoulder for another woman in the room.

"I'm going to be in Draywood tomorrow and was wondering if I could meet with you to talk about local real estate," she says.

"Of course, I'd be happy to help you. What time is good for you?"

"Eleven?"

There's a pause as he checks his calendar. "That works. Are you looking for a vacation home, or a year-round residence for you and your family?"

"Year-round. I'll give you the specifics tomorrow." She ends the call, not wanting to spend any more time than necessary on phony details.

She packs a full-size suitcase, not knowing how long she

may need to remain in the area. To make sure she won't have to find a laundromat, she includes a week's worth of clothing along with some warm winter outerwear. The altitude is considered below the snowline at 3000 to 3500 feet, but it could still turn frigid at night, and flurries are always possible.

At the last minute, she digs into the photo album for a portrait of Sadie taken not long before she disappeared. If Rebecca were to encounter a trustworthy resident who's been there for more than nineteen years, she could show them the photo and ask if they remember seeing a girl like her around town, or at anyone's house. This is a very long shot, but still worthy of an attempt.

It's late afternoon by the time she sets out. She listens to more podcasts about animal wildlife during the drive, though it makes her miss her friends at the refuge. When she stops for gas, she gets coffee to keep her awake since the monotonous drive through Central Valley tends to make her drowsy. She also buys a bag of chips to hold her till dinner.

It's about seven by the time she pulls into the motel parking lot. The place looks roughly equivalent to a Motel-Six, with design flourishes straight out of the 1950s, a big neon sign, and outside entrances for the two levels worth of rooms. She doubts they ever get close to filling the place, especially not now, too late for summer and too soon for ski season. Nor is there any major tourist destination nearby. All of this explains the near empty lot. She figures the two parked cars either belong to employees, or to people visiting relatives in the area.

Since the office is empty when she enters, she rings the bell. After a few minutes, a door to a back room opens and a boy emerges. He has freckles and long eyelashes and looks no more than sixteen. She assumes he must be older since he works in this place and doesn't appear to have parental control over his appearance, as evidenced by purple hair and full lower-arm tattoos.

He moves with nervous energy. "Good evening, ma'am."

Rebecca tries not to laugh. At twenty-five, she's not sure anyone has ever called her that before. "I have a reservation. Rebecca Danser."

"Is it just you, ma'am?"

"Yes, I'm alone."

"May I see your license and credit card?"

She slides them across and looks over the counter, where he inserts the card into a device connected to an iPad. His hands look too big for his arms, like they reached full size ahead of the rest of him.

He places the iPad in front of her. "Sign here, please."

She basically makes a line with her finger.

"Will you be staying past tomorrow?" he says.

"I'm not sure yet. Is that all right?"

"I don't know. We're expecting a busload of tourists from Hawaii."

She looks at him blankly, and he laughs. "JK, who would ever come here from there?" He returns her items and hands her an actual key, not a key card. "Room fifteen on the second floor. It's in the back. You can drive around and park there. Need help with your luggage, ma'am?"

She wonders just how old he thinks she is, and reminds herself to check the mirror as soon as possible. What if all this mindcasting is making her age prematurely, like a time-traveling *Picture of Dorian Gray*? Though actually, Dorian still looked young, it was only the picture that was a fright.

Declining the boy's help, she goes outside to her car, but when she turns and looks back through the glass, she sees him still standing there, watching her with a curious look in his eyes. It gives her a little chill, which she quickly shakes off, reminding herself she's grateful that although the motel looks ancient, thanks to this tech-savvy kid, she just had the fastest check-in ever.

Rebecca parks in back, gets her suitcase from the trunk, and carries it up the stairs. She has to jiggle the knob to get the key to open it. Inside it smells musty and the decorating is dated, with puke green carpet and tile in the bathroom that's the color of dried blood. At least from her quick inspection, the toilet and bed sheets look clean. It's good enough.

After freshening up and changing into a different blouse, she goes out. From her research she knows the few places to get dinner in town. She could order it to-go and eat in her room, but she figures it will be best to present herself in a public location as soon as possible, to reduce the amount of interest she might attract as she wanders through the area over the next few days. Most likely everyone else already knows each other. A stranger is bound to attract attention.

Since JJs Bar & Grill is only a quarter mile from the motel, she decides to walk. The so-called highway is more like a wide road with light traffic and sidewalks on both sides. She passes a gas station-slash-repair shop, a convenience store, and a building supply company. Eventually she spots the restaurant up ahead, its lights blazing like a beacon in the growing darkness. It reassures her to see vehicles in the lot, a sign that she's not the only creature remaining—along with the boy—in this post-apocalyptic town.

She steels herself before opening the door. There are so few choices of where to eat… what if the kidnapper is inside here right now? She prepares her face not to show any reaction before entering and pausing at the *Please wait to be seated* sign. Glancing around, she counts two families, four couples, three single diners. No Bob. She lets out her breath.

A waiter wearing a black bow tie over his flannel shirt approaches her. "One?" he asks.

Rebecca nods and follows the man to a table that's awkwardly too large, where he hands her the menu without comment. As she scans the list of entrees, she keeps an eye on activity around her. A gray-haired man seated alone is looking her way, but when she catches him at it, he shifts his gaze quickly. A little later, she notices an older waitress staring at her. But when their eyes connect, the woman smiles at her, holding her gaze until she's the one to look away.

After figuring out her order, Rebecca lays down the menu and checks her phone, not that there's really anyone in her life who would get in touch with her right now. A few minutes later, the waitress who was looking at her earlier approaches instead of the waiter who first seated her. The woman is past middle-age, but wears her hair in a ponytail and curled-in bangs that look childish on her. She's dressed in a pink blouse that ties with a bow at the neck, a straight, black skirt, and fat-heeled shoes.

"Hello, sweetie-pie. Can I get your order?" she says.

Rebecca masks her annoyance. She dislikes when someone she doesn't know calls her *sweetie*, or *honey*, or *darling*. "I'd like the grilled chicken with potatoes and red peppers," she says.

"Good choice. Anything to drink?"

"You have a local wine you can recommend?"

"Sure do. Laughing Duck pinot grigio will knock your socks off."

"I'll take a glass of that."

The waitress writes it down. "Your first visit here?"

"That's right."

"What brings you to our little town?"

"I just came for some fresh air," Rebecca says.

"You'll find plenty of that. Where do you hail from?"

"Bay Area."

"Well, I'm Patricia. I work here most nights. You have any questions about what to do around town, just come to me."

"Sure, thanks." Rebecca doesn't share her name.

"I'll get that food for you right away."

She wasn't lying about the food coming quickly. Though after taking a few bites, Rebecca thinks it might've benefited from more careful preparation. The wine is good, however. She works on a sudoku while she eats.

Later when the waitress takes her credit card, she scrutinizes it on her way to the register. Maybe she's supposed to do that when it's a stranger passing through town. But Rebecca has already decided she won't be coming back to this grill. Something about Patricia has left a sour tang in the back of her throat.

Chapter Sixteen

REBECCA GETS UP EARLY and goes for a run along the tangled roads in the area behind the motel. Homes are few and far between. Streets are narrow, winding, and full of potholes. There are no sidewalks but it hardly matters given the lack of traffic. It's darker than she expected, with light from the rising sun shimmering through the towering pines.

This day will be a challenging one, emotionally and perhaps in other ways as well. When she returns from her exercise, she takes a shower, and dresses in comfortable leggings, with a thin cotton V-neck top and her softest fleece jacket. She walks down the street for coffee and a donut from a tiny building where you order at the window because there's no room for seating inside. She takes it back to her room at the motel, happy to avoid the chance of running into Martin Ortiz before their appointment.

To ensure she arrives on time, she drives to his office though that too is within walking distance. She's a few minutes early when she pulls into one of the three spaces provided for parking. Inside, there's a small reception area with no receptionist, leading to three equally small offices. Two are empty and Martin emerges from the third with hand outstretched. "Thanks for coming. Come on in." When he smiles widely, revealing dimples and beautifully aligned teeth, she has to remind herself he could be involved in terrible crimes. Otherwise she would find it hard to resist the green eyes, the wavy black hair with an errant curl on his forehead, the two- or three-day shadow on his lips and chin, and the way his polo shirt emphasizes the swell of his arm muscles.

He leads her into his office to a comfortable chair by the window. "Can I get you coffee?"

"I'm caffeine'ed out, thanks." She glances around while he settles behind his desk. She's not sure she's ever seen such a neatly organized office. Brochures are stacked at matching heights. His business cards, pen holder, and stapler are lined up in a perfect column on the other side. There's a vase with matching orchids, all poised in a state of early bloom. She thinks they must be artificial.

"If you don't mind my asking," he says, "what brings you here? A new job for you or your husband?"

"I'm not married." She's probably only imagining that his eyes show a dash of increased interest. "I'm a writer. I can work anywhere, and I love looking out at trees. It's affordable here, compared to most parts of California. I don't know. I think I could grow to like it. What do you think?"

"Obviously I love it, since I live here myself. People are friendly, but it's remote. Quiet. You have to be comfortable with that."

"I could be. Why don't you show me what's available? Not too large. It's just me."

He stares at her, thinking. "There's a place that just came on the market last week. Beautiful lot, but accessible."

"Accessible?"

"That means not too far from the highway. Do you have time to see it? Better than looking at brochures. And it's empty."

"All right." She almost feels guilty for wasting his time, but then, she has an excellent reason for doing so.

"My car's in the back," he says.

When she rises, her jacket brushes the brochures, knocking the top ones off center. He carefully straightens them before leading her out to a sporty-looking Subaru parked at the curb. To her relief, he doesn't try to open the passenger door for her. She can't stand when guys insist on doing things she can easily do herself.

"I think you might love this place," he says, getting into the driver's seat. "It has a great deck and lots of privacy." He elaborates on the amenities during the ten-minute drive, but since it's all a ruse to learn more about him, she doesn't pay close attention.

When they draw up to the house, she realizes he wasn't exaggerating. The place is beautiful. Rustic but modern. Surrounded by mature trees that look as if they've received regular care and pruning. Just the right distance from the neighbors: too far for prying eyes, too close to feel scarily isolated.

She follows him inside, where it's sparkling clean, with stunning wood floors and bright painted walls. They go into the kitchen.

"Oven and stove are electric but you can convert to gas."

"Why would I do that?"

"Oh, a lot of people think food cooks better with gas."

"I don't cook."

"Really? You might want to rethink that if you're going to be living around here. There aren't a lot of takeout options."

"I'll keep it in mind. I suppose you think it's odd, wanting a house for just one person."

"Not at all. I live alone too. Well, me and my dog, anyway."

"I love dogs. What kind is it? What's your dog's name?"

"Her name's Galleta."

"That's pretty. What does it mean?" She moves through a hallway into the first bedroom.

"Cookie. Or, more like a biscuit. Doesn't matter. I like the word, but now I just call her 'Guy' all the time."

"Guy. That's cute." She could see herself picking a name like that. "But are cookies her favorite food?"

"She doesn't get to eat them, so I don't know."

"What is her favorite food?"

"Anything that smells like bacon."

She can hardly believe her good luck in getting this information out of him. He doesn't appear suspicious either.

"There's three bedrooms and two full baths," he says.

"Good. I can have visitors." She pauses. "Be honest. Tell me what it's like to live around here. I've heard you can get oddballs in these foothill communities."

"I guess you don't have any oddballs in Silicon Valley?"

She laughs. "No, we're all one hundred percent normal. Whatever normal is."

"To answer your question, yeah, we've got oddballs. But overall, it's a nice community. Friendly. But not intrusive."

"Have you lived here long?"

"All my life. Well, except when I was at college."

"Did you come home in the summers?" She hopes not, because that would be around the time Sadie was taken.

But he gives a little laugh. "Yeah. Yeah, I did. I guess I'm pretty provincial. I even live in the house I grew up in now. My father sold it to me when he moved to Central Valley."

"And you haven't filled the place with children yet?"

"I'm not even married. My girlfriend was living with me, till we broke up last year." He gives her a curious look. "You know, for someone who wants to live alone in the woods, you're pretty talkative."

She decides it would be wise to give it a rest. They go out back to view the deck, which truly does look like a wonderful place to sit out in the evening, listening to the breeze rustling the branches of the trees. If she ever did live in a place like this, she probably would want a dog, though. Or maybe two.

"Let me show you another place you might like," he says.

"Um, thank you, but I have a meeting this afternoon. Need to go back to my motel room to connect."

"Okay, sure." He leads the way through the house, pausing to restore doors, window coverings, and light switches to the state they were in when they arrived. "Does tomorrow work for you? I assume you'll be heading back to the Bay Area soon."

"Let me think about this one. I'll let you know if I decide to look at any others."

The drive back to his office is fairly quiet. She feels guilty in a way, taking up his time. He doesn't seem like he could be involved in Sadie's kidnapping. But she has to be sure.

She actually does go back to her room, afraid if Martin sees her around town she's going to look like a liar. Luckily she brought several novels with her. She picks the most promising and stretches out with it on the comfortable chair by the window. She reads all afternoon, quitting by eight o'clock or so, in time to get dinner.

Anxious to get to the business of this evening, she buys a pizza and brings it back to her room. When she's finished eating, she rises to close the shade on her window. Noticing a car parked across the street from the motel lot, she draws back and turns out the light in her room. It's an odd place for someone to leave their vehicle, with nothing around except an empty field.

She's about to shrug it off when the light of a cell phone flashes inside the car, illuminating a person sitting in the driver's seat. But before she can make out any details, like what gender they might be, the light goes off.

Rebecca lowers the shade and sits down. Could someone be watching her? She's not sure what kind of car this is, but it isn't a red Kia. If Reamer is still following her, he must be driving something else. But she doesn't believe he would come all this way. It wouldn't have been easy for him to track her on the highway for so long without her noticing. Besides, he isn't the kidnapper. She has begun to believe his purpose in approaching her before was as simple as what he claimed —he wanted her to know he had nothing to do with Sadie's disappearance.

But if not Reamer, then who? Has Bob noticed her around town, without her noticing him? How would he even know who she was? After struggling with this thought for several minutes, she decides it's possible he's looked her up and seen a recent photo on the Internet. Maybe he keeps tabs on her family, wanting to be sure there are never any leads in the case.

She gets up again and folds back the shade to peer out. The car is gone. On the one hand, she feels relief; on the other, she wishes she could be sure it had nothing to do with her.

Before getting into bed, she chains the door and pulls the heavy chair in front of it. But even with these extra precautions, it takes far longer than she had hoped to settle down and grow more relaxed. The real work doesn't begin until she's almost asleep.

Chapter Seventeen

REBECCA TRAVELS BACK in time to the morning of the same day, landing inside her less-than-twenty-four-hour-younger self just as she prepares to leave the motel.

This time she doesn't drive to Martin's office but instead goes to the market, where she purchases bacon-flavored dog treats. From there she heads directly to Martin's family home, which she expects to find empty, save for Galleta—Guy—the Great Dane.

It's just past eleven when she turns onto his street. He's now in his office waiting for her to arrive, and she hopes he'll give her at least an hour. She turns off her phone to ignore the inevitable polite call or text he'll make in fifteen minutes or so, asking if she is still planning to meet with him.

She knows the instant she pulls up in front of Martin's house that it isn't the one where Bob took her. The property is similar but much better maintained, surrounded by trees and somewhat remote from its neighbors. This home is also a sprawling one-story, as opposed to an overshadowing two.

It brings her some relief to discover another piece of

information that could clear Martin and his father of any involvement in Sadie's disappearance. But she can't yet discount the idea that her sister might've been taken here eventually. The involvement of the Ortiz family car in her kidnapping continues to be a damning detail.

Since Rebecca has come here via a mindcast she can afford to take more risks. She has already decided it will be necessary to get inside the house and search for any evidence of children being trafficked or kept as prisoners, or of a connection with the mysterious *Bob*.

Since there's no car in the driveway, she's hopeful no one else is at home. He said he and his girlfriend broke up last year, but a new one might have just moved in, or a relative, or a housekeeper. She should've asked more questions while she was with him, but she had been wary of raising his suspicions. Especially if he might truly have something to hide.

The best way is the direct approach, she decides. She rings the front doorbell, which causes a frenzy of barking to erupt from the backyard. Guy's register is low and deep, the kind that would scare intruders away if they didn't bother to go look at her. Great Danes are known for their gentle dispositions. Helen at the wildlife shelter, who used to breed them, told Rebecca the greatest threat they posed was the potential for whacking you with their whiplike wagging tails.

If anyone comes to the door, she has a story ready about confusing the address of his home and office. But no one does, even after a second ring. She waits a minute longer before trying the knob in case he accidentally left it open. No such luck, though.

She checks behind to make sure no one is watching before walking to the back of the house, rattling the treat box on her way to give Guy a preview of coming attractions. The dog is leashed to a long rope, allowing her full range of the yard from the back door to the edge of the forest. As soon as Rebecca rounds the corner, Guy bounds toward her, forcing a backward leap that keeps her barely out of reach. Her presence inspires another round of energetic barking.

"It's okay, girl. Look, I have treats." She opens the box and waves the smoky scent of bacon at the dog's nose. She grows quiet immediately and strains her head forward.

Rebecca tosses a treat that's caught in mid-air. "Good girl." She holds out the next one toward her mouth. "Gentle, Guy." The dog licks it off her palm and she keeps her hand extended to be sniffed. "See? I'm friendly." Guy allows herself to be petted now. "Good girl. What a beauty you are." The dog turns and presents her rump for scratching, a favorite spot for Danes. "You like that? Oh you're just a great big softie, aren't you?"

Rebecca is now free to cross the yard to the deck, pausing to pick up a tennis ball and toss it, not too far so it stays in Guy's range. The dog fetches it but instead of bringing it back for more throws, she settles on the grass chewing it.

Peering in through the back door, Rebecca scans the inside of the house. Sparsely furnished in a good way. Beautiful cedar floors. A stone fireplace like her family used to have. Is there a basement? She doesn't see any ground level windows, but there might still be something down there that they had specially built for potential appalling deeds. What if her sister is alive and a prisoner inside this house? Or what if another girl is being held captive now? The need to get inside and find out overwhelms her. Though it appears to be a normal house belonging to a normal man in a normal neighborhood, horrors might be hidden within.

This door is also locked, but unlike the front entrance, it

has window panes above the knob. Breaking the glass might be beyond Guy's level of tolerance, but she sees no other way. She spots a toolshed on the far side of the house and manages to find a pickaxe inside it. *Martin, you shouldn't make it so easy for burglars.* Before using it on the glass, she puts out the treat box for Guy. As soon as the dog is distracted, she takes a great swing with the axe and shatters one of the lower panes. She pokes at the glass, pushing it into the house, and reaches in to open the lock from inside. When she pulls back her hand, she discovers she's bleeding from one of the shards cutting into her. It's messy but not deep. She wipes the blood on her pants.

Guy jumps up to accompany her inside, but Rebecca slips through quickly and pushes the door shut before the dog can get in. No way is she going to take the chance of the shattered glass on the floor cutting into the poor girl's paws.

She washes her hand with soap and water in the nearest bathroom, and wraps a small towel around it. No time to go looking for Band-Aids. Martin might soon get tired of waiting for her and decide to pop home for lunch.

Her first goal is to search for a basement, and it doesn't take long to locate the door in the laundry room. She opens it, her nerves prickling, expecting to see a burned-out bulb hanging from a string like in every horror film she's ever watched. Instead, she's pleasantly relieved to find a normal light switch at the top of the stairs, and a modern light fixture at the bottom. Still, she can't help feeling a shiver as she calls down the steps. "Hello? Anyone down there?" It would've amazed her if a reply came, yet when it doesn't, she feels disappointed.

She starts down the narrow, steep steps that creak underneath her feet. Maybe fewer pancakes and syrup would be in order. At the bottom, she finds the basement consists of two sections. On the right there's a tidy workroom, with a table saw and tools hung on the walls. In fact, this could be the reason for the basement, which isn't a common thing to find in California homes. Martin's father was a carpenter and needed a workshop. It's possible Martin learned woodworking from his dad and continues to use this space.

On the left, there's a door. Again, that nervous feeling runs through her. As she grasps the knob, she calls out again. "Hello? I'm a friend. Don't be afraid."

She pushes the door inward to darkness, but the light from the hallway allows her to find the switch inside the room. The overhead fixture comes on and reveals a carpeted area with two armchairs. Several boxes rest along the wall on one side. On the other side, there's an upright piano with a bench. Sheet music rests open in front of the keys.

Rebecca isn't sure what to make of this room. It certainly is not being used as a prison for little girls now. But it could've been. It has its own door. There are no windows. The walls and floor are finished. Remove the piano and chairs and replace them with a bed and a table, and it's the same as the shed, only more spacious.

The boxes might tell her something. She opens the first one and finds it filled with novels, mysteries by authors like Agatha Christie, along with books for a younger age, like Nancy Drew. She pushes this to the side and opens the next. Her breath catches in her throat when she sees the collection of toys inside. Things that a small girl would like. Dolls. Coloring books. Crayons. Building blocks. She turns with some trepidation to the last box. Her hands tremble as she lifts out a girl's flowered dress, small enough to fit a four-year old. Frantic, she dumps out the contents of the box, and with growing panic, picks through the rest of the contents. There are t-shirts, leggings, socks, underwear, bathing suits, sweaters, and jackets, all clothing that a girl might wear, in sizes that would cover ages four up to ten or twelve.

Though she doesn't find the unicorn t-shirt and red shorts Sadie wore on the day she disappeared, it brings her to tears to imagine these are the clothes she wore, toys she played with, and books she read. This was her prison.

A sudden noise interrupts her thoughts. Footsteps on the stairs, rapidly descending. Her limbs turn to jelly while her breath sticks in her throat. Before she can think what to do, Martin fills the frame, his face a dark cloud. "What are you doing here?" The calming, resonant tone has sunk to a growl.

Nothing that comes to mind is believable, the truth least of all. She remains crouched by the box, silent, her thoughts racing for a means of escape. *I will not let him take me.* Even being a prisoner in the shed for such a short time was horrific to her. She'd like to mace herself for leaving the can in her purse in the car.

He enters the room. His hands are empty; he hasn't brought a weapon, thank god. When he's a few feet from the door, she makes her move. Springing up, she dashes to the exit, banging the side of him, knocking him against the wall. She makes it through to the stairs, takes them two at a time, races to the front door. She hears him bounding after her. As her hand touches the knob, he reaches her, wraps a strong arm around her waist, and the other around her shoulders. He literally picks her up, drags her back to the couch, and sits on her. "You're not leaving till you explain yourself," he says.

She's weeping, she can't help it, she's so afraid of what he's going to do to her. "Let me go, let me go," she cries.

"I could've called the police. I've got a camera out back,

you know. But a professional thief would look for that. Are you new to this? The camera and Guy are supposed to be deterrents. Admittedly, Guy sucks at her job."

It takes a few seconds for his words to sink in. Is it possible he really thinks she's a thief? She looks at his face. He almost appears as if he feels sorry for her.

"Why didn't you call the police?" *Because you don't want to attract their attention,* she thinks.

"I have no idea. Maybe because I couldn't believe what I was seeing? Also, Guy liked you, and she's a good judge of character. At least she used to be."

She decides to try a lie. "You're right. I'm a lousy thief. I lost my job and I'm out of money. I didn't think you'd have such good security out here in the sticks."

He stares at her like he's trying to read her mind. "Nope. I don't believe it. You're too smart. And this was too stupid. Why would you go in the basement? Hello? I keep cash in a drawer in the kitchen. I've got an iPad and a laptop in the study. Who keeps valuable stuff in the basement?"

Her mind races trying to make her lie sound real, but she's at a loss.

"You were going through the boxes my ex-girlfriend left here. Her daughter's old clothes that she hasn't bothered to pick up. What could possibly be of any value in there?"

His ex-girlfriend's daughter? Could this be true?

"Are you a friend of hers? Did she ask you to come get her stuff so she wouldn't have to come here?" He's basically talking to himself at this point. "But you only had to come to the door and I would've brought it out to your car for you."

He looks down at Rebecca, who's still refusing to talk, and takes out his phone. "Don't try to get away because if you do, I'll have to leap and tackle you to the floor, and that's really going to hurt." He enters 9-1-1 on the screen. "I'm going to report you unless you tell me what you were doing here." He raises his finger above the call button.

She can't be sure if he's bluffing. But she reminds herself she isn't in real-time. Mindcasts are for taking risks she wouldn't dare take otherwise. Mindcasts are for sharing information she wouldn't dare share otherwise.

"A silver Ford Taurus registered to your father was used to kidnap my little sister Sadie nineteen years ago," she says.

His face transforms. She has to admit, it would be extremely difficult to fake the level of astonishment he shows, unless he were one of the finest actors in the world. "What?" he says.

"Your father's car was used to kidnap my sister. That's why I'm here. I came to look for evidence of her having been held here. Finding a box of girl's clothing, toys, and books has definitely raised the probability."

He stares at her like he's trying to read whether she's lying or not. "If that's true about the car, why haven't the police ever been here?"

"I found out recently. I can't explain how. But it's true. Absolutely true."

He releases his grip on her. "Don't move or I'll tackle you, like I said." He gets out his phone. "What's your sister's name?"

"Sadie Danser. I'm Rebecca Danser."

His fingers move on the phone and he reads what's on the screen, his expression becoming grim. He does another search before pocketing his phone again. "What a fucking horrible thing to happen." He moves to the side of the couch, freeing her up. "You read about this stuff… you always wonder how the family manages to cope…"

"Not very well, obviously."

"If you want to leave now, go ahead. Just know that neither me nor my dad had anything to do with what happened to your sister. It turns my stomach just to think of it. And my dad… if you knew him, you'd know it's impossible he could ever hurt a helpless child."

She sits up but makes no move to leave. His offering to let her go weighs heavily in his favor. She can't believe he'd do that if he were guilty. "Why do you have a basement room like that, separated off with its own door?"

Martin lets out a small laugh. "You saw the piano, right? It was my mother's room. She was self-conscious about her piano-playing. Thought she wasn't any good and didn't want to drive anyone else crazy having to listen to her. After she died, my father didn't have the heart to change anything about that room. I didn't either. It's like a memorial to her."

His explanation, which came quickly to his lips, makes sense. Who would put a piano in a room meant to hold captives? They could be banging away on that thing any time someone came to the house, attracting attention.

"Could someone have borrowed the car?" she says.

His brows fold together in concentration. "No, I don't think so."

"It was a silver Ford Taurus, right?"

"Yeah. He had it for years."

"Could someone have stolen the plates… and put them on another silver Taurus?" Even as she says it, it sounds ridiculous.

"Weird to steal plates and put them on an identical car."

Something else occurs to her. If Martin is involved, this next question might seal her fate. But if he isn't… it's worth trying. "I have other information. The man who drove the car was young at the time. And the left side of his face was partly paralyzed."

Martin stares hard at her. It's clear this information triggered something inside him. "You sure about that?"

"Yes."

He gets up, walks across the room, pauses and runs his hand through his thick hair. "Tell me when this happened."

She gives him the date that's seared into her memory: July 28, 2000.

He nods his head. "It was that summer, I'm sure of it. I was back from freshman year at college. The carburetor was acting up and I took the car to the service station. This was early in the morning. He said he could do it right away and I walked home, planning to pick it up later. Then a little while afterward, he called my dad and said he wouldn't be able to get to it until Monday. Something about an emergency he had to deal with at home. Dad said, fine, we had the truck, so it wasn't a big deal to go without the car for a few days."

"Okay."

"But then on the Monday, when we got it back, we noticed a couple of things. First, the mileage. Dad had checked it a few days before we brought the Taurus in, because he was starting to think about selling it and wanted to see what it might be worth. So when we got the car back, he noticed it was hundreds of miles more than it had been. The second thing was the fuel level. It had more gas in the tank than when we dropped it off. Why would the mechanic fill up the tank?"

"Did you say anything to him?"

"You bet. My father went right over there and yelled his ear off. But he steadfastly denied using the car, and implied my dad made a mistake and didn't have the right mileage number or gas level. There wasn't any way to prove either one. So there was nothing we could do except take our business elsewhere. We never used his service station again, not even to buy gas."

A warm feeling of relief fills her, making her realize how badly she wanted Martin to be innocent. His story rings true.

"Please tell me the name of this service station owner," she whispers.

"Jeremy Toth."

Part IV

Chapter Eighteen

EVERY EVENING for the last four days, Nicki has brought a bowl of chicken noodle soup and crackers to Mother in her room. This time when she carries in the tray, she finds Mother looking the worst she has since the flu began. She lies flat in bed with her face pale and lined, her nose red, and her eyes half-closed. Used tissues overflow from the wastebasket beside her, and the top of her bedside table is crowded with cold medications, throat lozenges, a Kleenex box, a water glass, and a thermometer.

"I can't eat," she rasps. It sounds like laryngitis. "Call Uncle up here."

Nicki sets the tray on the dresser and hurries back out into the hall. "Uncle! Mother wants to talk to you." She remains leaning against the wall while his steps approach from the family room. He climbs the stairs faster than usual because Mother never likes to be kept waiting. When he goes into the bedroom, Nicki listens at the doorway.

"My temperature's a hundred and four." Mother erupts

into a coughing fit. When it ends, she says, "I might have pneumonia. You need to take me to Urgent Care."

"Okay. Right now?"

"Of course right now." This almost starts another coughing fit. "Nicki, bring my clothes."

Uncle waits in the hall while Nicki helps Mother change out of her pajamas into a long-sleeved shirt, sweatpants, and a zippered sweater. "Get my brother again," she says when they're done.

When he returns, Nicki retreats to a shadowy corner of the hall, hoping they'll forget about her.

The two emerge from Mother's room, with Uncle holding her purse and her leaning heavily against him. When they reach the top of the stairs, Mother pauses and looks back at her. "Go to your room, Nicki."

She swallows her disappointment and does as she's commanded. Uncle approaches behind her and shuts her door, locking her in.

Nicki listens carefully through the crack as they clamber down the stairs and out of the house. The car engine starts, and as soon as its sound grows distant, she erupts into action. *Now is the time.*

She empties the contents of Cinderella's butt onto her bed and gets to work on the door with the bobby pins. Having had other occasions to practice, she's gotten rather good at this. It takes no more than two minutes to open the lock, bringing with it a feeling of elation. But she can't delay, there's much to be done.

First, she changes into her *escape outfit,* as she's already designated it in her mind. Nights can dip to near freezing in November. A flannel shirt, her thickest jeans, her heaviest sweater, warmest socks, and sturdiest shoes. She takes out the only winter jacket that still fits her from the closet, along with a second jacket, the pink one she wore when she was younger, and one more sweater. These she lays on the bed for now.

From the pile of stuff, she pockets all the cash. She wishes there was far more, but it's been risky stealing as little as she has. Nothing could ever be swiped from Mother's purse, as the penny-pincher would be certain to notice. Only Uncle was forgetful enough not to miss a dollar here and a dollar there, which she snatched out of his wallet whenever he left it out of his sight.

She brings her list with her into Uncle's room, which she has never entered before in her life. She's glimpsed it from the hall many times when he's opened the door to go in or out of it. But no one, not even Mother, is allowed to enter, and surprisingly, she's always respected that.

It stinks of ripe garbage, and Nicki can see why. Used dishes are scattered across the room, on the bedside table, the dresser, a small table next to a chair by the window, and even on the floor. She has seen him carrying large piles down to the kitchen after they've accumulated for some time.

There's a wicker hamper in the corner, and this is piled high with dirty clothes, adding to the stench, no doubt. Likewise, his bed is unmade and it looks like the sheets haven't been washed in months. She wonders why he wants to live in such squalor, and why Mother tolerates it.

She dreads what she might find in the closet. The clothes hanging in there are cleaned and ironed, though. Mother does that for him. She supposes he must wait until he's almost out before delivering more items to be washed.

However, the other half of the closet is taken up by a bookcase filled with stacks of magazines. It turns her stomach to see the naked women pictured on the front covers. She looks away.

Forcing herself to check his dresser for anything useful, she's thrilled to discover the key to the shed in the top drawer. She had been expecting to have to use the bobby pins, but it was going to be hard outside in the darkness with no one to hold the flashlight for her. Also, it's a different kind of lock and she didn't know if she could work her magic on it. Finding the key makes everything faster and easier.

One other item that isn't even on her list strikes her—a baseball cap. It looks clean enough, probably because he rarely wears it. She tries it on, then adjusts the back to fit her smaller head. The cap will help disguise her appearance while they travel.

In the bottom drawer, she finds his gun and ammunition. She's heard him talk about it with Mother before. One time when they saw wild turkeys in the back, he wanted to shoot them. But she wouldn't let him, saying the neighbors might call the police, wondering what the crap was going on over here. *Crap* was Nicki's word; Mother considered that cussing and probably had said *heck*. They all had to put their hands over their ears whenever someone swore in a movie. Anyway, Mother told Uncle the gun was only to be used for their defense, like if a burglar broke into the house. Nicki couldn't imagine that ever happening. There was nothing here anyone would ever want to steal.

It flashes through her mind that she should take the gun to protect herself and Sadie, but just as quickly, she nixes the idea. She has no idea how to load it, never mind shoot anything. If she tried, the most likely outcome is her accidentally killing one of them.

At the same time, she doesn't want *him* to have it. He and

Mother might be so enraged upon returning and finding the girls gone, she might just order him to hunt them down and shoot them like they were rabbits. She pictures Mother dressed like a witch, putting them in a giant oven to be roasted for dinner.

Holding the weapon gingerly, like it's a bomb waiting to explode, she carries it to her room. *Where should I hide it?* Glancing around, she decides *under the mattress* will do. It will be easy to find if Uncle searches here, but she believes he'll be convinced she took it with her. Because that's what he would do. Then she realizes she must hide some of the ammunition as well, to complete the impression that she's traveling with a loaded weapon and might even use it against them if they come after her. It may make them hesitate.

The search for useful items continues in Mother's room, where the powerful odor of Vicks VapoRub lingers. At least it clears her nasal passages. She has snuck into this room several times in the past, not just when she stole the bobby pins, and knows Mother keeps a jewelry box in her dresser. Nicki has no idea whether any of it is genuine or just cheap imitations purchased from garage sales, but that will be for the pawn shop to decide. Emptying the box onto Mother's favorite scarf —which is supposed to be silk and probably really is—she ties it up to make a pouch.

Stealing from Mother goes against all her instincts. It feels like a violation and a betrayal, because Mother has spent many years applying layer upon layer of guilt. *I went through hell giving birth to you. We work our fingers to the bone. Why? To pay for the house and everything in it so that you can live comfortably. To provide you with all the food your tummy desires. To buy books for your useless education.*

She claps her hands over her ears to shut out Mother's

voice in her head. Nicki is only doing what is necessary to save Sadie. They'll need cash and her dollars and coins won't last long. She has an idea how much things cost from seeing receipts for groceries and other purchases, and from listening to Mother and Uncle talk. They have never once given her money of her own, since she's not allowed to go anywhere. The children she watches in movies or reads about in books often get an allowance. They're able to go out and make friends and live full lives. How is it fair that she's been denied these freedoms?

Her thoughts steel Nicki for taking the jewelry. At the same time, she prays she's not found and brought back here, because Mother will punish her for it till the end of time.

Once she's added the new things to her pile on the bed, she returns to Mother's bedroom for one more item of significance. During a previous snooping expedition, she discovered her own birth certificate inside a file cabinet hidden behind Mother's dresses in the closet. She has since learned from her reading that a birth certificate is an important document that's required for identification when a person applies for a driver's license or a passport. She actually can't imagine ever going to other countries where she'd need a passport, but she would like to drive a car someday.

She brings the document back to her pile and continues downstairs to the front closet, where Uncle keeps his backpack. After dumping out its contents on the floor, she recovers a utility knife with its own sheath from the mess and restores it to the pack. Then it's on to the kitchen, where she fetches the map from the junk drawer. She's studied this hard in the past whenever she found a few minutes alone in the kitchen, so she knows the general direction they plan to take, but the farther they get from the house, the more she'll need to rely on the map for reference.

A pair of Mother's sunglasses catches her notice. She tries them on and they fit pretty well. Between these and the baseball cap she'll have a decent disguise that will hopefully keep strangers from guessing how young she is. She puts them with the map in an outer pocket of the backpack.

Nicki takes all five water bottles remaining in the kitchen, hoping they'll last till they can reach a convenience store in another town. As for food, most of what they eat at home is frozen. But she takes the rest of the sliced bologna and American cheese, a bag of carrots, half a loaf of bread, an unopened box of Cheetos, and a package of Oreos.

Coming to the end of the list, she returns upstairs to pack everything she left on the bed. She places the birth certificate inside a plastic bag so it will have extra protection in case the pack gets wet. She adds her thinnest, lightest blanket to the top, along with the extra sweater and jacket, ready to be handed over to Sadie. Putting on her own coat, she pauses to think hard regarding anything else they might need. At the last minute she remembers her watch. It's a cheap thing they gave her for her birthday once, and she never wears it around the house because who wants to be reminded of time when they have nowhere to go? She finds it stuffed in the back of her drawer and makes sure it's working before putting it on.

No more time to waste. They might return any second. Mother might suddenly feel better and call off the visit. Or Urgent Care could be closed. Or Uncle might drop Mother off at the hospital and come home without her. One could not count on them following through on any plan.

She grabs the flashlight and spare batteries on her way out the back door, switching on the light as her feet crunch on pine needles. A drip of water lands on her forehead and she looks up at the solid bank of clouds overhead. It might be the first rain of the season, just her luck. She increases her pace to the shed and lets herself in with the key.

Sadie is crouched in the corner with her arms wrapped protectively around herself as Nicki enters and sprays the light on her. Seeing it's Nicki and not Uncle, she lunges forward and hugs her tightly. It stabs Nicki in the heart to think of her alone all this time. "I'm sorry. They wouldn't let me come before," she says.

"I missed you," Sadie whispers. "Becca and Mr. Fluffernutter missed you too."

Nicki kneels down beside her, slips off her backpack, and takes out the sweater and jacket. "I have good news. We're leaving here. Tonight. We won't have to be separated ever again."

She picks up Becca the rabbit and presses her into the pack. Sadie looks past her through the door. "Are we going in the car?"

"No. We have to go through the woods. I have a map. There's a back road, not too far."

Her eyes grow damp with fear. "The woods? Are Uncle and Mother coming?"

"They're not here now. Mother is sick. Uncle is taking her to the doctor." Nicki picks up Mr. Fluffernutter the dog. "We're running away."

"No!" Sadie screams. "No, we can't run away!" Tears start to roll.

Nicki pauses and grasps her twiglike arms. "It's okay. I've planned it all out. We'll be okay."

Sadie is hysterical. "They'll catch us and bring us back and hurt us!"

"We won't let them catch us." Nicki is not at all sure about this, but she tries to exude confidence.

"They'll hurt my mommy and daddy and my sister Becca if we're bad!"

"I know they told you that. But that's not going to happen. Your family is safe in their own house. They aren't here. Mother and Uncle can't get to them."

"How do you know?"

It's a good question. It's true she can't be sure. Uncle might find his gun or buy another. He might be crazy enough to go to Sadie's parents' house and try to shoot them.

But she can't allow Sadie to talk her out of this. She's a little girl and doesn't understand. Nicki is older and it's up to her to save them both. Dying is better than living as prisoners.

"Listen to me." Nicki makes her voice as calm as she can. "You know I love you. You know I won't ever allow you to come to harm. We have to get away from them. They're bad and we can't trust them. We'll run away and find your mommy and daddy and you'll have a real life again."

Sadie sniffs unhappily.

"Can you do this for me? Can you be strong for my sake? Because I can't live here with them anymore. But I can't leave you behind either."

"I don't want you to go without me," Sadie says.

"Okay, Good. We go together." She stuffs Mr. Fluffernutter into the pack. "It's cold out there." She helps Sadie put on the sweater and jacket, zipping it for her and pulling up the hood. Then Sadie gets on her sneakers with the Velcro fastenings.

Nicki swings the backpack over her shoulders and takes Sadie's hand. "We can do this. You're like my sister and sisters are strongest together." They walk out side-by-side and Nicki shuts the door behind them, hoping to delay the moment when Uncle or Mother notices they're gone.

Nicki switches the flashlight back on. "This way." Sadie clutches her free hand as they hurry toward the trees in the back. Lightning flashes directly in front of them, followed by a deafening blast of thunder. Rain cascades over them.

Chapter Nineteen

AS USUAL, Rebecca does not wake till morning. She must've returned right after learning Bob's real identity—*Jeremy Toth*—and slept soundly through the rest of the night. Having an actual name for him at last must've given her the feeling of resolution that brought her back to her own time.

Moreover, she feels a powerful sense of satisfaction in being nearly certain Martin had nothing to do with it. She quite likes him; she can admit that to herself now. She wishes she could make him a full ally by confiding in him, but years of false leads have made her cautious. Present day Martin knows nothing of what just happened in the alternate past, and she needs to keep it that way.

The first thing she does upon rising is Google Jeremy Toth of Draywood. This is sufficient to reveal his home address and the location of the business he owns. She realizes with a shock that it's the service station just down the road from the motel, the one she walked past on her way to JJs the first night.

Anxious to confirm that Toth really is Bob, Rebecca skips

the morning shower, gets dressed, eats a granola bar she finds in her purse, and drives to the service station, hoping to find him on duty. It's one of those little independent stations one hardly sees anymore, a combination of two gas pumps and a small repair shop. She eases in next to a pump, shuts off the car, and peers through the front window. No one is visible at the register or in the garage. He could be using the bathroom, or doing paperwork in a back office.

Since the station doesn't even have a credit card scan at the pump, it gives her the perfect excuse to tromp right inside and see him up close when he comes out from hiding. Thinking about it makes her uncomfortable as hell, but it needs to be done.

The door dings as she enters and shoots her gaze across the two aisles with her stomach doing somersaults. It takes a minute, but finally she hears steps approaching and sure enough, *Bob* wanders in from a side door that connects to the repair shop.

It's definitely him, though the signs of paralysis on the left side of his face are slightly less pronounced than before. Having lost hair and gained weight, he looks twenty years older than when he tossed her in the back of Martin's Taurus, but it's still unmistakably him.

Seeing her staring, his expression stiffens and it's like a veil drops over his eyes. She figures people have been staring at him all his life, and at times, brutally mocking him for a condition he might've had since birth. Under normal circum-stances this would evoke her sympathy, but her heart holds nothing aside from hatred and disgust for this beast.

"It's just me working here," he says, choosing to interpret her look as one of impatience. "Can't get to the register as quick as I'd like."

His name badge identifies him as Jeremy, in case she had any doubts. Not trusting herself to say anything, she takes out her credit card and looks for the card reader where she's supposed to insert it.

He holds out his hand. "Leave it here. I'll charge it after you fill up," he says.

Her throat goes dry as she stares down at her name on the card. Surely after stealing Sadie, he followed the news about it and therefore knows her last name and probably the full name of everyone in their family. *Stupid, stupid, stupid.*

"Wait, I might have cash." But like a lot of people her age, she rarely carries any with her. He watches as she opens her wallet exposing the empty billfold, recalling how she'd meant to stop at an ATM but then forgot.

Somehow she finds herself handing over the card, thinking who looks at it anyway? And he doesn't look at it, just sets it beside the cash register and shifts his gaze to the front window like there's something interesting to see outside, which there isn't.

But if he wants, he'll have all the time in the world to check out her name while she pumps gas into the car. Heading back outside, she berates herself for handing the card over and for forgetting to bring cash. She needs to be thinking further ahead. She's already made so many rooky mistakes. Her stomach churns the whole time while she fills her tank. Right now, he could be looking her up on the Internet, checking her photo for a match, confirming that she's sister to Sadie who was taken when she was four. By Bob the Kidnapper, otherwise known as Jeremy Toth.

Her hands are trembling when she pulls the nozzle from her tank, making her spill a bit of gas. Grabbing a paper towel, she wipes her hands over and over, dragging her feet back into the station to retrieve her card. He's already rung up the sale and wears a bored expression as he holds out the card and receipt for her. He says nothing and avoids eye contact, which just about confirms her fear that he now knows exactly who she is.

She can't get out of there fast enough, though she has to stop a few hundred yards down the highway to set her GPS to Toth's home address. Service is spotty, but it should get her there. She prays he doesn't anticipate her next move by closing up his shop and driving home to thwart her plans. She'll have to take that chance.

She heads up the mountain and within twenty minutes, the GPS tells her to turn right, just as she remembers from when Toth kidnapped her. There's a street sign identifying it as Pinyon Road, the right address. She hesitates whether to turn onto it, not wanting to attract attention from the neighbors or to accidentally drive too near Toth's house. On the other hand, an unfamiliar person walking down their street might draw more stares.

She makes the turn and passes several houses that are widely separated from each other, like a lot of places in this area. The one closest to the highway has been updated recently with light pine accents and is truly beautiful. But the others look unchanged since whenever they were built, maybe fifty years ago. Trees hug them close and cast dark shadows. She hopes the people who live in them are mentally well-balanced and not Unabomber wannabes.

Before long she comes to a mailbox with Toth's street number stuck onto it. Rebecca pulls over, peering down the long driveway, barely able to glimpse the roof of the house at the end of it. She'll have to park here, though if Toth does come home, he'll know instantly that she's at his house. She knows what she's doing is impulsive and dangerous and downright crazy, but a wild urgency has gripped her and she can't stop herself.

She's half-walking, half-running down the driveway, not even looking around, just focused on getting to the house as quickly as possible. Minutes later, the trees open up and the steep-roofed building she remembers appears before her, with the old wooden garage next to it. Without doubt, this is where Toth brought her. There's no pickup parked on the side this time; maybe Jeremy drives his truck to work. No other vehicles are in the driveway either.

Glancing up at the house, she searches the windows for movement, or the silhouette of a person looking out. She thinks there might be a light on in one of the upstairs rooms, but she can't be certain in the daylight, and anyway Toth could've left it on by accident.

Nothing can hold her back now from dashing between the garage and the house toward the clearing in the back. When she comes around the corner, she sees the dull gray shed exactly as it was nineteen years ago, perched on a rise, conveying a sense of forsaken solitude and isolation that fills her heart to breaking. Its high window—the one where she fell over trying to reach it—faces this side. *This is it, this is it.*

She sprints across the messy yard past piles of leaves and stacks of logs, mindless of the noise she's making, branches cracking, pinecones snapping beneath her feet. When she reaches the door, she rattles the knob and yanks at it with both hands, but it won't come open. She raises her arms and pounds her fists against the wood. "Sadie! Sadie, it's me, Rebecca, your sister. Speak to me. I've come to save you. Tell me you're there. Please, please, say something." She crumples to her knees and presses her head to the door, weeping.

All is quiet inside the shed. Most likely, no one is there. But it's also possible Toth has frightened and brainwashed Sadie—or some other girl now—so thoroughly, she doesn't dare call out for help.

Though Rebecca wishes she could take a sledgehammer to the place, now isn't the time. She forces herself to turn away, to retrace her steps to the car. As she passes the house, she looks up at the upper window again and wonders if there's a flash of movement, like someone drawing back so as not to be seen.

She's quite sure that if someone is there, they will not call the police to report her for trespassing. But they might well burst out of the house armed with a gun, prepared to shoot her down. It might even be within their rights to kill tres-passers; she isn't certain of the law. These thoughts bring with them a spike of adrenalin, and she runs faster than she ever has toward her Honda, weaving as she goes to evade a speeding bullet if one comes behind her.

When she flings the car door open, she glances back without seeing anyone, but still she doesn't pause except to whisk up the keys after she drops them. Her breathing is ragged as she starts the car and drives away, trying hard to keep herself from flooring the gas. When she turns back on the highway, she lets out a cry, though she doesn't know whether it comes of despair for not finding Sadie alive, or triumph to finally have discovered the place where she was taken and who took her. To be so close at last to finding justice for her sister.

After reaching the downtown area, she parks near where she plans to grab coffee and brunch, and spends several minutes doing deep breathing exercises to calm herself. When she trusts herself to speak again, she calls Freddie.

His message says he'll be on vacation until two days from now. "Call the office if you need someone to help you before then," his message continues. "Otherwise leave a message and I'll get back to you as soon as I return."

Fuck. She leaves a short message asking him to call when he gets back, knowing he won't check it while he's away. He told her once he never gave out his personal phone number for exactly this reason. When he's on vacation, he wants to be on it one hundred percent.

She briefly considers contacting the local police department. But without any real proof, aside from, *I travelled back in time*, she won't be able to convince anyone to investigate Toth's background, let alone take out a warrant. Freddie should at least run a check on him like he did on Daniel Ortiz, Martin's father, and if something turns up in his past, the detective might be willing to go further than that, maybe even drive out here and help her. There might be DNA evidence inside the shed or the house. She just needs to convince Freddie, but now it's going to have to wait two days.

Chapter Twenty

AFTER FILLING her stomach at the breakfast café, Rebecca takes a long walk through a heavily wooded neighborhood near downtown. It truly is a beautiful community, and under normal circumstances, she wouldn't mind living here, except her tendency to isolate herself would become even worse.

But mostly during the walk, she thinks about how she will nail Toth. She needs to time travel, of course, and she can do it tonight. She'll mindcast back to this morning when she drove out to his place and find a way to get into the shed. Its one window is too high up, and too small for her to fit through anyway. She'll have to break into the house, even if it means shattering more glass. Once inside, she might as well search the whole place for any evidence that Sadie has been there. Hopefully the key to the shed will turn up in the process. Toth being at work should give her plenty of time for a thorough going-over.

It's possible, though, that a friend or relation of Toth's might be living there too, and she needs to be prepared for that. This is why she brought the mace and duct tape. She's never used either one against a person before, but now isn't the time to shrink from unpleasant tasks. Of course, she'll do her best to avoid confrontation. She didn't do well trying to fight off Martin. Not at all. But then, she wasn't prepared. Even the dumbest thieves—the candidates for Darwin awards —probably knew to check for cameras before breaking in anywhere, but this never occurred to her, even though her own apartment building uses them. Even if she hadn't noticed she was being filmed till she was already on his property, at least she would've known she only had a few minutes to search before police and/or Martin arrived.

Her phone rings while she's trying to decide if she should turn back from her walk. *Martin.* She's not sure if she should answer, until she remembers she's in real-time now, and everything that took place between her and him at his house happened during a mindcast. Sometimes she has trouble keeping track of which experiences occurred when.

Real-time Martin thinks Rebecca came here to purchase a house. He's probably calling to show her another place, or ask if she's still considering the first one. Feeling bad wasting his time, she decides to make an excuse.

"Hi Martin," she says.

"Hey. How are you?"

"Good. Enjoying a beautiful walk on a quiet street. I suppose you're wondering about my decision?"

"No. I mean, yeah, but that's not why I called… I don't generally do this sort of thing… shit, that sounds like such a line. Let me start again. Do you want to have dinner with me tonight? I'm not asking as your real estate agent."

She hesitates. Should she? She basically has nothing to do for the rest of the day, until she gets into bed and travels back in time to search Toth's house. It's not a matter of availability.

But is this wise? She doesn't want to form any obligations. Nor does she want to hurt him by leaving him in the dust as soon as she gets Freddie to come help her.

"Yes," she says, surprising herself. "That sounds nice."

"Great. I can pick you up or…"

"I'll meet you there."

He gives her the location before hanging up. She hopes she doesn't regret this. She hasn't had a date since before she started mindcast-sex with Dev. Seeing someone in real-time creates expectations. The longest relationship she's ever had lasted three months, and it was eleven weeks too long. She can't stand having someone rely on her, like a boyfriend would. She can't bear to be in a position of letting anyone down. Not again. Not ever again.

When all this is over, she'll find another sex buddy. Not Dev. The last time they were together, she decided she didn't really like him. But maybe Martin. He's growing on her. Come to think of it, it's good she accepted the dinner date. That's more than she ever had with Dev. She can find out if she enjoys Martin's company. If so, it would add a new dimension to mindcast-sex. Maybe they'd even take time to have a meaningful conversation now and then. Not in real-time, however.

The more she thinks about it, the happier she is that she accepted his invitation. She's always led an isolated life, but here in *Sticksville*, she feels lonelier than ever. And more frightened. It's scary to think she could be the only person in town who knows the truth about Toth. Especially since he may be aware of her identity now. If anything happens to her before she speaks to Freddie, Toth could get away with everything.

After she's turned back and nearly reached her car, a

familiar-looking older woman with bangs and a ponytail approaches Rebecca.

"Hello," the woman says. "I hope you're enjoying your visit." Seeing the blank look on Rebecca's face, she adds, "I'm Patricia. Your server at JJ's?"

"Right, I remember." She pictures her at the restaurant the first night, wearing an old-fashioned blouse with a large bow. "Yes, thanks, my visit has been very… productive."

"Oh I thought you were here to enjoy yourself. I suppose you're one of those people who hangs on her computer."

"I wouldn't say that." She steps past the woman.

"Are you coming to JJ's tonight?" Patricia says.

"Not tonight." To be nice, Rebecca adds, "Though the food's very good."

"If you're thinking of getting dinner somewhere else, you can't go wrong with Wild Mushrooms in Yellerton. It's just a twenty-minute drive down the highway. Everything on their menu is delicious."

"Thanks for the recommendation. I'm dining at another restaurant there, but I'll keep that in mind for tomorrow." She opens her car door.

"Have a lovely evening," Patricia says, turning back the other way.

After returning to her hotel room, Rebecca notices right away that the maid has been there. The bed is made and items have been straightened. The counter has been wiped and new towels supplied. But when she opens the drawer where she put away her clothes, it appears her things have been moved. She's quite sure she placed her black leggings on top, meaning to wear them tonight. But they're at the bottom of the pile.

Why get into the drawer? Maybe the maid is a thief, but

she doubts it. They wouldn't last long here if they pilfered from the customers, and word that they were fired for stealing would whip through town faster than a California wildfire.

Rebecca checks to see if anything's missing, but she doesn't think so. Aside from clothing, she also left the duct tape, the photo of Sadie, and the printout of information on Martin in here. She should've taken those last two items with her, she realizes now. Any doubt Toth had regarding her identity would've been erased by Sadie's picture. Even worse, on the printout it says "Kidnapper's car" at the top, right above Martin's father's name and the address of their family home where Martin now lives. Below that she has notes about where Daniel moved, what Martin does for a living, and the location of his office. At the bottom she had added the name of his dog and her affinity for bacon.

A chill sensation grips her. Toth could've come here any time during the last few hours. He might have a helper at the station, and he also doesn't seem to mind closing up the place when he feels like it. Of course he would check this motel for her; where else would she be staying? Naturally he would know the young office worker along with everyone else in town. The kid would think nothing of revealing all he knows about the hotel's latest guest.

She checks the door for signs of anyone messing with the lock, but it looks normal. Not that she would be able to tell the difference if Toth picked it with a credit card, or if the kid let him borrow the key. She opens the door and glances out. The maid is nowhere to be seen. Cleaning wouldn't take long with no more than one or two other rooms occupied right now. The maid has probably left for the day.

Rebecca shuts the door and sinks onto the bed, thinking. She has to assume Toth has seen her page of notes and knows she's aware the Ortiz family car was used in the kidnapping. It occurs to her this knowledge might also put Martin in danger. More so because he has no reason to be wary of Toth. What happens in a mindcast stays in the mindcast, meaning present-day Martin doesn't know any of the things she told him during her visit to his home in the recent past. It may be best to fill him in during their date tonight.

Rebecca is the much more likely target, however—a thought that makes her shiver as she contemplates how the lock on her door is no deterrent to Toth. What can she do to dissuade him from coming after her? Maybe let it be known that she's "working" with the police. Actually, Freddie still doesn't even know where she is. When she left her message, she said nothing about her location. If he knew she'd come chasing after the owner of that car, he would be angry and unwilling to listen to anything she had to say. He might not even return her call.

Chapter Twenty-One

REBECCA BLOCKS her door with the armchair again before taking her shower. It's getting dark early these days, and she has no idea if Toth would take the risk of coming back to her room while she's here. She hopes if he's that crazy, this will block him long enough for her to call the police.

Turning her thoughts to Martin, she takes extra care with her preparations. No question he's her type and if this was the seventeenth century she'd probably swoon when he entered the room. Nothing will come of it tonight, but she can allow herself a little pleasure just looking at his handsome face and sexy male body. What she would really like to know is, just how hot does he think *she* is? Because that would really help her decide whether he's the right choice for her next round of mindcast-sex, whenever that might happen.

But she never in a million years thought she might meet a guy she liked on this trip, which is why she doesn't have anything stunning to wear tonight. She wishes she had her little red dress, though it might've been over-the-top for a first date. She has to settle for her black leggings and plunging off-white top made of light cashmere. And sneakers because that's all she brought for her feet, and her slate blue puffer jacket because the night is sure to get cold. At least she has one pair of dangling silver earrings and a diamond stud to add some sparkle.

After leaving the motel, it takes longer than she expected to reach the next town down the mountain and find street parking near Anthony's Organics. She's ten minutes late when she walks in and finds Martin waiting by the door. He gets up and touches her arm lightly by way of greeting. This was exactly the right move, because she hates being hugged or kissed before a first date even gets started.

"Do you want to sit outside? They have heaters."

She glances toward the patio, visible in the back. "Sure, that sounds nice."

They follow the hostess out the screen door to a table that overlooks a garden. The heater is on and Rebecca sits close to it. There's a lit candle and roses on the table, colored lights strung across the patio, and no one else seated near them. The ideal setting for romance.

The menu is mostly vegetarian, partly vegan, and has a wide range of food types from several different countries. She hones in on the Thai avocado curry, which sounds delicious if not quite authentic. "Do you only eat vegan?" she says.

He shakes his head. "I'm a vegetarian, but I don't have the will power to cut dairy and eggs from my life."

"I don't blame you. I'm mostly vegetarian, but I don't even have the will power to cut poultry or fish from my life."

He smiles as he adjusts the roses in the vase, and the positioning of the candle beside them.

"I can see why you became a real estate agent," she says.

He glances up. "This, you mean?" He nods at the items on the table.

"You obviously have an eye for detail."

"That's a nice way of putting it. I'm obsessive about things."

She shrugs. "It's better than not caring, if you ask me." That might be her flaw. Too much apathy, except for the single obsession that's driving her life at the moment. Something to work on eventually, if she can raise enough interest to do so.

They make small talk while waiting for the server to take their order. When he's left them alone, Rebecca says, "You're probably wondering what I've decided about the house."

"I don't want to rush you. That's not why I asked you out."

"Then let's not talk about it." She had been about to reveal the real reason she came to Draywood, but she stopped because it would put an end to any chance of having a pleasant dinner together. She knows from experience that *my sister was kidnapped nineteen years ago* is an absolute mood-killer.

"I have a game I sometimes play when I meet someone new," she says. "We tell each other something about ourselves, and the other one gets to guess if it's true or false."

"How do you know if they're telling the truth about whether it's true or false?"

"You have to trust each other. And I guess you could Google it later." She smiles.

"I'm game. You start."

"Hmm." She glances up at the dark sky, thinking. "I played the bagpipe from age ten to twelve."

He scrutinizes her. "Are you part Scottish?"

"No clues."

"Then I say you're lying."

"Yeah, I wanted to, though. I was fascinated by all things Scottish at that age." The waiter arrives with their wine.

After he's poured and gone away, they raise their glasses and clink them. "To… fulfilling our dreams," Martin says.

"For the record, playing the bagpipe is definitely not one of my dreams anymore."

"I won the county spelling bee in 7th grade." He takes a sip of wine.

She purses her lips. Could he be a former child geek? But there's something in his eyes that makes her think he's lying. "False," she says.

"I have dyslexia. I'm terrible at spelling. Though not that bad for someone with dyslexia."

Their appetizers arrive, distracting them. As the meal progresses, the conversation moves to what they like to do for exercise, for hobbies, and then for work. "You said you're a writer," he says. "Can I find a book of yours at Barnes & Noble?"

She laughs. "I'm not a published writer. Not even an agented writer." It's tempting to add, *not a writer of any kind, actually*.

He's silent for a moment.

"I know what you're wondering. How is she going to afford the house?" she says. "Man, you're looking at a trust fund baby."

The waiter returns to ask if anyone wants coffee or dessert.

"Not me," Rebecca says, thinking the caffeine will interfere with her upcoming mindcast.

"I'll take the check, please," Martin says. He turns back to

Rebecca. "True or false. My mother died of cancer when I was twelve."

She's confused at first, thinking he's already told her his mother is dead, though he didn't mention how. But that must've been during her mindcast. It seems unfair that she already knows the answer, yet she feels certain she would've known this wasn't a lie.

"True," she says softly.

He nods. "I just wanted to tell you. It affected me more than anything else in my life. So, I wanted you to know."

"My little sister was kidnapped when I was six," she says.

His brow tightens as he looks at her, reading her, knowing she's sharing with him the same thing—the trauma that's affected her more than anything else in her life. "I'm so sorry," he says.

A silence follows as they leave the restaurant and he walks her to her Honda. On the way, his arm slips around her shoulders. When they reach the car, he wraps both arms around her and holds her tight. "I can't think of anything more heartbreaking than losing your sister like that," he says.

"It changed everything about my life. I think about her every day. It's worse, far worse, than if she'd died. At least then we'd know her fate. It's the ghastly stuff I imagine that... Do you know the story of Prometheus? How Zeus punished him for giving man the gift of fire? He was chained up and an eagle would come to eat his liver, which would immediately grow back so it could be eaten again the next day. This is how it feels to have someone you love taken from you, and each morning the first thing you remember is that."

He doesn't know what to say. How could he? She's never shared this part with anyone before. "I can't believe I just told you that. You probably think I'm demented." If he knew about the mindcasts, he would definitely think so.

"Then I must be too, because what you said made perfect sense to me."

He gets it, probably because he also had overwhelming grief to deal with as a child. This is when she makes up her mind to tell him everything. She draws back and says, "I'm not planning to buy a house here at all. That was just a ruse."

He almost seems to brighten. "A ruse to…? I wish I could believe it was a ruse to land a date with me."

"Sorry. I'm not handling this well. It was a ruse to find out more about you but not for the reasons you hope. It's because of… um, because of an anonymous tip I received. A phone call from someone disguising their voice. The person, I think it was a 'he,' named the kidnapper and the man whose car the kidnapper drove. This informant said he was dying and didn't want this hanging over him anymore. He gave no explanation of his own role, or anything else. Just the names. And then he hung up, before I could beg him to tell me more or to come forward and talk to the police." She takes a heavy breath. "The car belonged to your father."

He stares at her in disbelief. "That's impossible. This tip you got, it's bullshit. If you knew my dad, you'd know how insane that is."

"The caller provided a detail no one outside of the investigators could've known."

"I don't care. It's still bullshit. Who did he name as the kidnapper?"

She lowers her voice. "Jeremy Toth. He owns the—"

"Christ, I know who he is." He takes a moment to think about it and settle his thoughts. Slowly, he relays the exact story he told Rebecca in the past. How they had stopped bringing their car to Toth after he apparently drove it somewhere when he was supposed to be repairing it. "It's possible," he concludes. "I can't tell you how disgusted that makes me to think our car might've been used that way. What are your next steps?"

"I'm waiting for Freddie—a detective who was on the case—to get back from vacation. In two days. I may have enough to get him to act, especially with your information."

"Maybe you should go to the local police right now."

"It isn't enough. An anonymous tip. And only your word to go on that your car may have been used without your consent. No proof of anything. It'll be hard even for Freddie to get something going. Local police would just alert Toth of our interest. He'd probably get busy destroying any remaining evidence." She has to be ready with incriminating details before the police are brought in. She needs to find them tonight, when she uses her time travel super power to go back, get into the house, and search for clues.

"It's your call, of course. When you're ready, I'll be happy to tell them what I remember. I know my dad would be willing to come here and talk to them too."

"Thank you."

He rubs her shoulder. "You gonna be okay? Come to my place tonight if you want. I'm not putting the moves on you. I have a spare bed. You like dogs?"

"I do. Thanks for the offer, but I'm okay." His presence could make her time travel difficult or even impossible tonight. And she can't delay it.

"Call me tomorrow," he says. "If you don't mind. I want to know you're okay."

"Sure. Thanks again."

He waits while she gets into her car and drives away. She would've liked to go with him. But she has to finish this.

By the time she returns to the hotel she's feeling exhausted. It isn't that she expended much physical energy, but the emotional toll is heavy. She's relieved to see the lot empty and no cars parked across the street as she turns into a space below her room.

When she gets out of her Honda, and pauses to lock it, the sound of footsteps behind her comes out of nowhere. Before she can turn, something hard is smashed against her head. Her mind goes blank as she tumbles to the pavement.

Part V

Chapter Twenty-Two

IF ONLY MOTHER had fallen ill in the middle of summer, on a still, warm night with zero chance of the clouds opening up and drenching Nicki and Sadie. But no, she chose to get sick and go to the doctor at the worst possible time.

Without having gone far, they're as soaked and shivering as if they had jumped into a cold mountain lake. Sadie's teeth chatter noisily, though she continues trudging alongside Nicki with astonishing determination. Their pace is too slow, however. Nicki keeps glancing over her shoulder for the signs or sounds of pursuit. Not that she's likely to see anything in the rain-soaked darkness, or hear anything over the steady pelting of water.

The thunderous explosion that accompanies a series of lightning strikes causes Sadie to fling her arms around Nicki, her eyes wide with terror. Nicki holds her tight, fearing the next one might land even closer.

She should've thought of these dangers. She should've been much better prepared. She should've realized she hadn't the slightest clue how to survive beyond the four walls of her house. The house that had protected her all her life.

They are lost. She knows that now. When she looked at the map, it appeared all they had to do was walk in a straight line from the shed across the stretch of woods that would end when they came to a narrow road. It was no more than half a mile away and looked like hardly any distance at all on paper. But she should have known that in the dark, with trees closing in all around them, there would be no way of telling what was *straight* and what was *walking in circles for hours on end*.

The flashlight isn't helping. It produces only a narrow beam of light, and not enough for her to differentiate one tree from the next. Not enough to tell if they've passed this particular tree before or not.

The brush is thick. She had hoped they might find a deer path or something leading to the road, but no. In some sections she has told Sadie to hang onto her jacket behind her, while she batted at branches and kicked at bushes, trying not to let anything poke them in the eyes. Already she has a tear in her parka from one of the sharpest sticks. At least it didn't cut her.

"I want to go back," Sadie says in a faint voice.

With a sinking heart, Nicki realizes they can't go back, even if they wanted to. They're surrounded by darkness. She has no clue which way leads to the house.

But she knows when something is futile. They could kill themselves wandering around in the dark, hardly able to see anything even with the flashlight. Already she nearly walked off a steep incline, which could've broken her leg at the least. And if Sadie had followed her, tumbling to the bottom, Nicki never would've forgiven herself.

"We'll find shelter." She begins looking for anything that

might serve. A cave would be nice, except she's not sure if bears might hibernate at this elevation. Usually they liked it higher up, but she had seen bears on the property on two occasions, the second time a mother with her cubs. She decides they will not be going into any caves.

But before long, she notices a large pine tree they may have passed earlier, with thick branches spread wide and low to the ground.

"Come here, Sadie." She leads her under the branches right up to the trunk.

"The rain isn't too bad here." It drips through the gaps instead of dumping on them. "Let's sit down."

"Do we have blankets?" Sadie says.

"Just the one." Nicki could kick herself for not packing more, but she'd run out of space in the pack. "Let's spread the pine needles first." She makes as neat a pile out of them as she can with her bare hands. But when she takes out the blanket, she finds it's nearly as soaked as the outside of the pack. "We can't use it. It'll just make us colder."

Sadie's face sinks as they settle on the pine needles.

"Let's eat something," Nicki says. The first thing she reaches, the Cheetos box, is soaked and soggy. She ignores that and takes out the bread, which was partly protected by the plastic. She assembles a sandwich with bologna and cheese, and hands it to Sadie.

"Not hungry."

"Are you sure? You should try to eat. You'll feel better."

"I don't feel good. I'm hot," she says.

Sadie's teeth were chattering only a short while ago. Swinging from cold to hot is not a good sign, Nicki knows. Putting down the sandwich in her lap, she reaches her arm around Sadie and draws her forehead to her lips. The girl is burning up. "Yeah, you're kind of hot," she says, not wanting to panic her. She gives her a water bottle from the pack. "Drink some of this."

While Sadie slowly sips, Nicki eats the sandwich, followed by three Oreos that managed to remain dry. She drinks from another bottle.

When they're done, she puts everything away, except for Becca and Mr. Fluffernutter. She gives them to Sadie, who wraps her arms tightly around them.

The cold is creeping up on Nicki inside. Like everything else, she woefully underestimated how low the temperature would dip in the foothills at night in the fall. She puts her arm around Sadie and draws her and the stuffed animals close. "We'll keep each other warm."

Sadie, with beads of sweat on her forehead, says nothing. After several moments of silence, they hear the crack of a twig breaking like someone stepped on it. "What's that?" Sadie whispers.

"It's probably just a squirrel or something." She prays it isn't Uncle coming after them. If so, they'll have no choice but to return with him.

"What if it's a bear?" Sadie says.

"They live up the top of the mountains. They don't ever come down here," Nicki lies. Still, she doesn't think it's a bear. A bear would make more noise.

"You sure?"

"Yup. I doubt it's any bigger than a raccoon. And they won't hurt us. We're safe here." She injects a confidence into her tone that she doesn't feel.

Hoping to distract Sadie, Nicki addresses the stuffed rabbit. "What do you want to be when you grow up, Becca?"

"A rabbit," Nicki says in Becca's voice.

"You already are a rabbit. I mean, what do you want to do?"

"Why didn't you say that the first time? I want to be a magician so I can pull a human out of my hat."

Though Sadie's face is pale and drawn, she smiles.

"What about you, Mr. Fluffernutter?" Nicki says.

"Hem, I would like to be a firefighter," Mr. Fluffernutter answers.

"That's very noble of you."

"A dog would never leave a burning building without leading his, hem, best friends to safety."

"You mean people?"

"Indubitably," the dog says. "We also like fire hydrants."

"I want to be a dog when I grow up," Sadie says in a voice so weak, Nicki can barely hear her.

"Why is that?"

"Because my owner would love me and take care of me and never let me be sad."

Nicki tears up at this and kisses her hair. "I want to be a doctor when I grow up. I'll love my patients and take care of them and never let them be sad, if I can help it."

Sadie closes her eyes and leans against Nicki. Before long, Nicki's eyes shut too and she falls asleep from exhaustion, despite the rain and cold, and her own fear and anxiety.

Dawn has broken by the time she wakes. Something feels off, and she realizes it's because Sadie no longer rests against her arm. Nicki looks around wildly, but doesn't see her anywhere. Sadie is gone.

Chapter Twenty-Three

AS CONSCIOUSNESS RETURNS TO REBECCA, she becomes aware of a throbbing ache inside her head, an uncomfortable pressure over her mouth, and a burning pain running through her wrists, arms, and shoulders. When she tries to move her hands forward, she discovers they're securely bound behind her back.

Wherever she is, it's utterly dark save for a sliver of light coming from the gap beneath the door. She's lying on her stomach on a hard mattress, her face turned sideways and something—probably duct tape—stuck across her mouth just below her nose. Toth has taken her prisoner.

She can't be in the shed because this mattress isn't on the floor, it's on a bed frame. Plus if that's sunlight under the door, she ought to see it shining in from the upper window as well. This has to be a room somewhere inside Toth's house. Likely it's still nighttime, and a light has been left on in the hall. Still, his house is nearly as cold as the shed might be. Since he didn't bother to put a blanket over her, she only has her light puffer jacket to warm her, and it isn't nearly enough.

What are his plans for me? She can hope she's too old to be of interest to him. He likes little girls; he preys on the young, the weak, and the innocent. He's deranged.

He must want her alive, though, because otherwise he would've killed her in the parking lot with multiple blows to the head. After that he could've driven straight home, burned his clothes, and buried the murder weapon anywhere in the forest around their property. Barring an eyewitness, they wouldn't be able to pin anything on him, even if Martin came forward with the information she'd given him. Since there was no proof of any of her assertions, Toth would get away with his crime. Again.

But he has let her live, for now. He must have a purpose. Most likely he wants information from her. How did she figure out it was him? Who has she told? How much does she really know? Eventually he'll come to ask his questions.

In the meantime, she must try to escape. Shifting her body toward the edge of the narrow bed, she suppresses a groan at the pain shooting through her. She swings her legs down to the floor and stands on wobbly legs. At least her ankles aren't tied so she'll be able to walk.

She moves slowly, barely able to see anything. Maybe he didn't lock her in, counting on her being unconscious all night. When she reaches the door, she has to grasp the knob with both hands behind her back, but it refuses to turn. She tries pulling the door toward herself in case it's not fully closed or the latch is disengaged, but this also fails. The door is securely locked.

Looking around, she finds her eyes adjusting to the darkness. She edges her way to the left, her fingers gliding along the wall, before she comes to a wooden chair and small desk with nothing on top of it. She wonders if there might be something useful in the drawers, but with her hands bound behind her back, it's impossible to reach inside them. Above the desk there's a window with a heavy shade drawn over it. In attempting to raise the shade, she pulls down but then loses her grip, making it fly upward with a loud snapping noise that she prays wasn't heard outside the room.

She turns her gaze to the porch lit backyard—the pine-needle-strewn clearing with the shed as its centerpiece. Could Sadie be in there now? As crazy as it seems, Rebecca refuses to give up hope of finding her sister alive.

Pressing her forehead against the glass, she peers down, wondering if she could escape through this window. But she's on the second floor; it's too high up. If she had the use of her arms, she might find a way to climb down. As it is, she wouldn't be able to do anything but fall straight to the ground and probably break an ankle, knee, or most likely her neck.

She continues her survey of the room along the perimeter till she reaches a closet, its door partly ajar. This too is empty, except for a few hangers with nothing on them. Assuming Sadie is alive, this couldn't be her room. There would be clothes at the very least. She doubts Toth could've cleared out everything of hers so quickly.

Rebecca returns to the bed with her head pounding and her body exhausted by her efforts. She lowers herself onto her side—a painful position but better than lying on her stomach. Thankfully, she sinks into sleep before long.

The sound of a key rattling in the lock wakes her the next time. Opening her eyes, she blinks at the shaft of sunlight that cuts across the floor from the window.

Toth lets himself in, shutting the door behind him. His hair is mussed and his clothes wrinkled like he slept in them last night. *Good*, she hopes he was miserable.

He carries a water bottle and wears a large knife in a holster on his right side. His gaze shifts to the open shade but he makes no comment on it.

She tries to speak but it's all garbled due to the duct tape.

He says, "I'll take that off so you can drink. But if you give me any trouble, I'll put another one on. It won't come off again. Anyway, screaming won't help. The neighbors are a long way off. They can't hear a thing. Are you going to behave?"

Once she nods her head, he steps toward her, grasps the duct tape with two fingers, and yanks it off. She cries out, feeling like she just lost a layer of skin. When she licks her lips with her tongue, she's relieved not to taste blood.

"Open your mouth, I'm going to give you some water."

She does as he commands and lifts her chin, but he pours too fast, making her choke. "Slow down," she says, her voice coming out hoarse.

He does as she asks, while looking annoyed about it.

"I'm starving," she says after finishing the bottle.

"Are you? I might feed you later, if you behave yourself."

"I need to use the bathroom."

He nods toward a bucket in the corner that she hasn't seen till now.

"I don't think I can use that when I'm all tied up like this," she says. "Can you free my hands? I can't get out of here with the door locked anyhow."

"No." He forces her down on her back with her arms pressed behind her. "Why did you come nosing around my house?"

Her heart thumps wildly. "Because you kidnapped my sister." There doesn't seem any point in pretending she doesn't know.

"Who told you that?"

"No one. I found out on my own."

"How?"

"I travelled back in time and watched it all happen." *The beauty of time travel is you can tell the truth and no one will believe you.*

He pushes against her already pain-filled shoulder, bringing tears to her eyes.

"Who knows you're here?"

"The police."

"Why'd they let you come snooping around all by yourself?"

"They weren't sure if they believed me. But now that I'm missing, they'll be here soon enough."

"Why aren't they here already? I think you're lying. Nobody knows where you are or why you came."

"Where's Sadie?" she cries out, unable to hold herself back.

"Don't know who that is."

"If you hurt her, you'll never get away with it."

"I never hurt anybody."

"Then why am I here? You're hurting me. I beg you, tell me what happened to her." She might never get another chance to ask these questions.

Saliva drips from the paralyzed side of his mouth and lands on her neck. "I said I don't know who you're talking about."

"Yes you do, you sick bastard. How many other girls have you taken? Weak little children who had no chance of defending themselves. You're a coward and a monster."

He takes out the knife and points it at her chest. "Shut up! You don't know anything!"

"You need help. Your mind is sick. A normal person

wouldn't do these things. Let me help you. Let me get you to a doctor."

"I said, shut up." He hesitates like he can't decide whether to kill her right now or not. Then he thrusts the knife back in its sheath. "Remember what I told you," he says. "You make a sound and I'll be back here with the duct tape."

"Please, please, tell me where Sadie is."

"She died years ago." He walks to the door. "You came here for nothing."

The way he says it, so unconcerned, so like he thinks her sister is nothing. The way he might talk about losing his pet chameleon. This causes a deep well of rage to rise up inside her. She makes a guttural sound in her throat as she lands on her feet and runs toward Toth. Moving quickly, he slips through to the other side and slams the door shut just as she reaches it. She pounds her head against it before collapsing on the floor, curled in a twisted heap, filled with impotent fury, listening to the sound of the key turning in the lock.

Eventually, she returns to the bed. But just as she's about to lie down, she notices several strands of her hair that must have come out when she was sleeping there. If she leaves them, they'll be easy for Toth to clean up once he's disposed of her, which is almost certainly his plan now that he's admitted killing Sadie.

But what if she hides the hair? What if Freddie comes looking for her, gets a warrant, and has the place searched? She needs to insure they find her DNA.

It's a painstaking job to work with her hands tied behind her, picking up a strand at a time, and depositing it some-where hidden inside the room. She drops one in the corner of the closet that would be hard to reach with a vacuum. Another in a desk drawer, blowing it to the back where Toth will be unlikely to look. A third one she lets fall next to the bed and then presses it right up against one of the legs using her foot.

Pushing through her exhaustion, she stands back against the plain beige wall that looks uneven in spots, like it used to be wallpaper and they just painted over it. She rubs her head against it until more hair comes out. She has to kneel down and fall over on the floor to retrieve the strands and stick them into her back pocket. Maybe she'll find a use for them later. When she's done, she struggles onto her feet and flops down on the bed at last. Ready to fall asleep and send her mind back to yesterday morning, before she came here to see the shed. She thought she may have glimpsed someone in the house, and if so, she needs to find out who that person is and what role they might be playing in Toth's crimes.

Chapter Twenty-Four

REBECCA SPINS through time and lands inside her day-old self just as she is stepping out the door of her hotel room. As sometimes happens, the abrupt transition makes her stumble and grasp the rail to steady herself. At the same time, a wave of relief washes over her at the realization that the agonizing discomfort she was feeling across most of her body has now disappeared.

She returns to the room to retrieve the duct tape and small pair of scissors she packed in her suitcase. These go into her purse underneath the mace, which needs to be the first thing her hand touches when she reaches inside.

Since she knows Toth is at the service station, she can skip that step and go directly to his house. This also gives her the advantage that if he does have a co-conspirator at home, this time he won't know to phone them and warn them about her possible arrival.

Same as before, she parks down the road from his driveway and takes it on foot. As she nears the house, she decides her best approach is to simply go to the door and ring the bell. If she were to try and break in, it would immediately tip off the person inside—if there is one—to the fact that she plans to make trouble for them. She hopes coming to the door will throw them off guard.

There's no doorbell, just a metal knocker that Rebecca raps three times. She waits with her hand at the top of her open purse. Several minutes pass while she wonders if she'll have to break in after all. If she could be sure no one was home, she wouldn't mind; it's the uncertainty that's frightening her. She knocks three more times, harder than before.

Finally steps approach from inside and the door opens a crack. A woman of around fifty or sixty with curled bangs peers out. *Patricia*, the waitress from JJs Bar & Grill, who somehow keeps crossing Rebecca's path. She's surprised and yet not surprised. The woman gives her a creepy feeling.

Patricia brightens like Rebecca is her best friend and opens the door wider. "Well, my goodness, you found me. Did you come to get those sightseeing tips I promised you?"

"Um, actually, I'm here to see Jeremy. I wanted to talk to him…" Remembering he's a car mechanic, she adds, "…about my Honda. Do you, um, work here?" Because it's hard to picture using the mace against this feeble-looking woman, Rebecca hopes she might just be the housecleaner or… she can't imagine what. Though Patricia seems like a phony, it's difficult to imagine her having anything to do with the murdering pedophile Toth.

But the woman laughs. "Work here? This is my house."

"Are you… are you Jeremy's wife?" She has heard of serial killers' wives having no idea of the crimes their husbands were committing. Patricia looks at least ten years older than Jeremy, but the age gap is the least of her problems if she's married to him.

"His wife? Oh no. I'm his sister. Why don't you come inside? As it happens, he'll be here soon. He forgot his cell phone this morning."

This isn't what Rebecca is expecting at all. Did he really forget his phone? He didn't look like he was going anywhere when she saw him at the station. But if he's on his way, she ought to get inside and prepare to mace him when he walks in. "Sure," she says. "Thank you."

Patricia gestures toward a chair. As Rebecca turns toward it, she feels something hard poke into her back. "This is a gun, and I'll use it if I have to, sweetie-pie. Walk down that hall. I'll be right behind you."

Fuck. She should've maced her. Now Patricia is probably planning to lock her in the prison room. She has to act now, or she'll be no better off than she is in the future. Whirling around, taking Patricia by surprise, she knocks the gun from her hand, whips out the mace and sprays it right into the woman's face. She screams, covers her eyes, and tumbles backward trying to escape another stinging blast.

Rebecca grabs her and pushes her into a kitchen chair. "Sit still or more mace," she says. Patricia lowers her face into her hands, moaning, while Rebecca tapes her to the chair. She doesn't cover her mouth in case she needs to ask her questions. But she does dampen a kitchen towel and presses it over the woman's eyes to help relieve them.

She doubts Toth is on the way, but to be safe, she takes the gun and the mace with her as she begins a rapid search of the house. Saving the kitchen for last, she moves out to a sitting room with a faded couch, old-fashioned TV, and stacks of movies on videotape. A dining room with a rickety table. A half-bath with a chipped mirror and rusty faucets.

Upstairs, the first door has a lock on its knob. Her skin

tingles as she wonders again if maybe Sadie had been kept in this room at some point. He told her Sadie died long ago, but why should she believe him? He wouldn't want her to know if her sister was still alive and being held captive. *Sadie, sweet sister, are you here?* Her heart sinks once again as she slowly opens the door and finds the room empty. It looks just as it does when they imprison Rebecca inside, missing only the bucket they must've brought later.

She crosses to the window and opens it wide, leaning forward to fling the gun as far as possible into the woods at the edge of the property. Since this isn't real-time, she's not going to worry about anyone finding it. She just wants it out of the way because she isn't going to use it, not even during a mindcast.

Continuing down the hall, she comes to a bathroom and then another bedroom. It smells like shit, with dirty dishes scattered all over the place and clothes on the floor. She checks the closet, where issues of Playboy and Penthouse are piled up. Toth's room, obviously. It makes her want to puke.

She searches the room without regard to the mess she's adding to his own. In his bottom drawer, she finds more ammunition for the gun. But there's no law against owning one, especially if he has it properly registered, and she finds nothing else in his room that might indicate criminal behavior. She even forces herself to flip through the magazines looking for child porn, but it's all adult women.

The third bedroom upstairs obviously belongs to the sister. Rebecca goes through her things with as much disregard as she displayed for her brother. She's about to give up hope of finding anything interesting when she gets to a small file cabinet behind Patricia's dresses in the closet.

Scanning through the documents, she learns the sister's

full name—Patricia *Gaunt*, not Toth like Jeremy. Maybe they're half-siblings or the woman was married. It doesn't appear there's any other man living in this house; at least, Rebecca hopes not.

The documents include the deed to the house, car titles, and old bank statements. Nothing interesting on first glance. But in a folder at the back of the second drawer, Rebecca finds a photo of a little girl.

Her heart constricts while for a fleeting moment, she thinks it's Sadie. She might've continued to believe this if she hadn't seen her quite recently. The girl has similar features, and appears to be roughly the same age as Sadie was when she disappeared, but her hair is darker, shorter, and wavier. It definitely isn't Sadie.

Toth must have a type, she thinks. This could be another child he kidnapped. If only she could take the photo back to real-time when the mindcast ends, but it isn't possible. She stares down at the girl's face a moment longer, trying to memorize it. *I won't forget you.* If, after returning to the future, she manages to escape from the prison room somehow, she won't leave the house without this picture.

Taking it with her to the kitchen, she holds it up for Patricia, who glares at her through watery, red-streaked eyes.

"Who is this?" Rebecca says.

Patricia turns her face away.

Rebecca aims the mace at her. "I said, who is it?"

"My daughter. Nicki."

"Where is she?"

"Not here."

"Tell me unless you want more mace."

"She's gone. She's never coming back."

"Is she really your daughter? Or another child kidnapped by you and your brother?"

"I don't know what you mean."

"Where is my sister Sadie? What did you do to her?"

"I don't know what you're talking about."

Driven by rage and frustration, Rebecca raises the mace to spray Patricia again. But before she can complete the action, the dizzying symptoms of her time travel coming to an end overwhelm her.

Chapter Twenty-Five

REBECCA'S MINDCAST was interrupted by the cold metal pressure of Toth's knife pushing up against her Adam's apple. She opens her eyes to find him sitting on the bed next to her, with his lopsided face bent over her.

"You make a sound, this goes straight through your neck," he hisses.

Someone must be here. She holds her breath, straining to hear any sounds inside the house. A minute later, a rapping comes at the front door. Toth grips her arm with his other hand, hurting her. After a short pause, a man's voice can be distinguished. *Martin.* Patricia must've opened the door to him.

Rebecca's heart melts at his concern for her. They only met two days ago, and here he is, searching for her, trying to learn why she disappeared from the motel and hasn't answered his calls. He isn't like any man she's ever met before, and she wants so hard to cry out to him, but she believes Toth is desperate enough to carry out his threat. Worse, if Martin finds out they've taken her it could put his own life in jeopardy. Patricia has a gun that wasn't thrown out the window in real-time.

The conversation is too muffled for Rebecca to make out what they're saying. Patricia must be putting on her act of folksy friendliness and helpless innocence. She'll pretend not to have ever heard of Rebecca or Sadie Danser in her life. She'll pretend Jeremy isn't home. She'll be a convincing liar, and Martin will have no choice but to leave. Rebecca doesn't think he'll go so far as to force his way into the house. Not for someone he only just met, who might be mentally unbalanced given the crazy story she told. God knows, anyone else would have already decided Rebecca had a whole set of screws loose.

Sure enough, the conversation ends quickly. Shortly afterward, Rebecca hears Martin's car start in the driveway. He's leaving, taking with him the last bit of hope inside her. She didn't know it would hit her this hard. She's reached the end.

Toth withdraws the knife and stands up.

"He'll be back," Rebecca says with more confidence than she feels. "He'll bring the police."

He ignores her, going out and locking the door behind him.

She hears Patricia coming up the stairs, and then her words. "It has to be tonight."

They'll kill me tonight and there's nothing more I can do. She's weak from pain and gnawing hunger. There's no escape from her bindings. No escape from this room. For the umpteenth time, she fervently wishes she could go back and really change the past, not simply observe it.

She regrets none of her actions, though. She found the monsters who did this thing to her sister. She doesn't think they'll get away with her murder. Freddie will come, and

Martin seems determined to help. She'll have to die, but her death will lead them to solve Sadie's disappearance. Toth and Patricia will be arrested and put in jail for the rest of their lives. This is her hope and solace.

She lies in miserable pain and sadness for hours, until the room begins to darken. She must've grown drowsy at last, because she suddenly feels her head heating up, and her vision blackening, like a new mindcast is beginning. The odd thing is, she usually has to be focused on it, concentrating on a particular time and place. But she suspects her subconscious is driving this. Her inner need.

When she arrives in the past, she and Martin are leaning against her Honda following their dinner together, and she has just told him about Toth and the role Martin's family car played in the kidnapping. Her first impulse is to throw her arms around him and tell him how grateful she is that he cared enough to come looking for her. But she holds herself back, afraid of confusing him. Afraid of scaring him off with her bizarre behavior.

The pain and hunger she was feeling in the bedroom prison are erased again. In fact, she's satiated from the delicious meal she just finished eating. They're almost at the point where she says goodnight and drives back to the motel, but she can't let that happen now. As soon as she leaves his side, there will no longer be anything to keep her in this reality, and she can't bear the thought of returning to that desolate room in which her life is surely going to end soon.

"Do you want to do something now?" A strange excitement pulses through her.

"Sure. You have something in mind?"

"Another game. I know, I'm full of weird games. I want you to imagine today is my last day alive. What would you show me in this town of yours? What would you recommend I do?"

He stares at her. "Should I be worried? Have you been threatened by Toth, or anyone else?"

"No, it's just a game."

"Because if you have, we should go to the police."

"I'm fine. This is just an exercise in making the most of each day."

He still hesitates.

"If you don't want to play, I get it," she says.

"No. It isn't that. I'm just worried for you."

"I'm not worried. If I've learned anything this year, it's that you can't stop the forward motion of time. Though you might pause it for a bit." She smiles to reassure him.

He thinks for a minute. "Okay, then. Carpe diem and all that. I've always tried to live that way. Experience every day as if it's your last… I've got an idea."

"Don't tell me," she says. "I want to be surprised."

"C'mon then. We have to drive there."

They go in Martin's Subaru. At the highway, he turns east toward Draywood, but when they reach the small town, he drives past it, climbing higher and higher into the mountains.

Already she feels better, enjoying the evening ride along the winding road. Magnificent trees on both sides of them. A man she respects seated beside her. A comfortable silence —an understanding—between them. And a surprise to come.

After forty-five minutes, they've left the lights of civilization behind them. Martin peers forward, searching for something. "I think this is it," he says a minute later. He turns the car down a dirt road, following it until it ends abruptly, blocked by forest. Martin shuts off the engine and pops open the trunk. "Here we are." They get out and walk around to the back.

Everything in the trunk is organized inside a basket stretched across the width of the car. Jumper cables, a collapsible snow shovel, a toolkit, spare water and snacks, maps, blankets, and more.

"Looks like we'll be fine here for days," she says.

"Weather's unpredictable in the mountains."

She gives him a crooked smile.

"What? You don't think this is normal?" he says.

"I wouldn't know."

He takes a blanket and uses his phone light to lead them to the start of a trail. Rebecca follows close behind using her cell, and before long they reach the top of a hill, where a vast meadow opens out in front of them. At the far side of the clearing, above the tips of the trees, the silhouettes of mountain peaks loom sharp, jagged, and infinitely fascinating.

"It's an incredible view," she says.

"C'mon, there's more."

They walk till they've reached the center of the meadow, where he spreads out the blanket. "Do you trust me?"

She can't remember the last time she trusted anyone. But when she searches for the answer inside herself, it emerges as a simple, "Yes."

"Lie down flat on your back, then." Once she's settled, he lays down beside her, with both of them gazing up at the night sky.

"The stars," she says. "My god, the stars."

"You have to go some distance from civilization to view them this well. And there has to be no moon."

"I've never done this before. I've never seen stars this bright. This distinct. There's so many of them."

"It's something everyone should get to see…" he trails off.

…*before they die*, she finishes inside her head. "Thank you for this." It could not have been a more fitting choice for her last night alive. "I suppose I should feel inconsequential compared to all these enormous and magnificent stars, planets, and asteroids. But actually I feel the opposite, like my life has been meaningful. Like I've made my imprint on the universe. Because here we are, living parts of this all-encompassing thing. We've had our roles to play, and who knows, if we'd never been born, the world might've been different in some small but significant way."

She wonders if when she's dust, her consciousness will merge with the universe. This seems all the more likely, given that she already has the power to separate mind from body and fly through space and time. All because of a spark from a mysterious rock. She wonders if it came from a planet of time-traveling wizards who probably have no idea what role they played in her life.

"We're interconnected in mysterious ways," she says. "I wouldn't be here with you now… I wouldn't ever have met you… if Toth hadn't used your father's car."

"Then it would've been better if we'd never met."

"I see it this way. A plant is fertilized with shit, but out of that excrement comes something beautiful and unique and living. I couldn't prevent him from kidnapping Sadie, but I can still welcome this precious feeling that grew out of a dark and sinister place." She shifts closer and slips her hand inside his.

They lie together under the brilliant stars until the cragged fingers of real-time pull her back.

Chapter Twenty-Six

THE RAIN HAS ENDED and the sky is rosy with the light of dawn when Nicki rises in a panic.

"Sadie!" She hisses the name, aware of the danger that Uncle might be out searching for them at first light. "Sadie, where are you?"

Nicki stares down at Becca the rabbit and Mr. Fluffer-nutter the dog, abandoned on the ground. If Sadie had set out to find her way back to the shed, wouldn't she have taken them with her? Hopefully this means she only stepped away to relieve herself.

Nicki emerges from under the branches of the tree and scans the area. "Sadie!" she calls again. The leaves stirring in the breeze provide the only response. She widens her search, checking for footprints in the muddy sections. When she finds one, she grows excited until she realizes it's too large for Sadie and must've come from her own foot last night.

Nicki pauses to consider where Sadie might've gone. Her fear of being caught by Uncle after having run away may have driven her to try to find her way back to the shed. She might've chosen not to wake Nicki because she knew her friend was set on running away and would insist on Sadie remaining with her.

On the other hand, Nicki's first instinct that Sadie might simply have needed to pee could still be right. Only if that was the case, she must've wandered too far and now she can't find her way back. Or, after losing herself, and maybe calling out for Nicki, she might've been discovered by Uncle and taken back to the house.

As the sun's rays poke above the treetops, she gets her bearings. To reach the road, located to the east, she would need to face the sun and walk toward it. She could leave right now and set a much faster pace than would be possible with a four-year-old at her side. A sick four-year-old, no less.

But inside her heart, she knows she can't go without Sadie. She won't be able to live with herself if Sadie is back at the house, being kept prisoner inside that tiny room. If Sadie is the one who has to face the punishment for the escape attempt forced on her by Nicki. Mother and Uncle will make her suffer for it.

With a terrible feeling of resignation, she turns away from the sun and heads west. It doesn't take long before she glimpses their chimney above the highest branches in the distance.

But when she lowers her gaze, a patch of pink color next to an aspen tree catches her eye. Rushing forward, she finds Sadie's parka lying on the ground, abandoned. The air is crisp and cold; why would she take it off? None of this makes any sense.

Nicki resumes her search with new urgency, circling outward from the aspen, until suddenly she finds Sadie curled up behind a bush, her eyes closed. Nicki drops to her knees beside her. "Sadie," she whispers, "Sadie, get up, we need to go."

But the little girl doesn't move or open her eyes. Her face is unnaturally pale and feels like ice when Nicki touches it. With a deepening sense of dread, Nicki shakes her body gently. "Wake up, Sadie. Wake up." When she lifts Sadie by the arms, the girl's head falls limply backward and Nicki lowers her again. "Sadie, no…"

Tears roll down Nicki's cheeks as she looks down at the one person she loved unconditionally. How will she carry on without her? It must've been the fever, she thinks. Sadie must've caught whatever Mother had. Maybe she'd been sick for several days without receiving any treatment. Maybe she wandered away in a delirium last night. She might've grown hot from the fever and thrown off her jacket. Afterward, she would've become cold. The night had been freezing; there was frost on the moss when Nicki got up. Lying here without a coat… the cold must've killed her. That, and hopelessness.

She's not sure how long she cries, but eventually she gathers herself, determined not to let Sadie's passing be for nothing. It's their fault she's gone—Mother and Uncle, who left her alone in the shed, sick and dying, while Mother was rushed to the doctor. Nicki must leave now, before they can find her, and put as much distance between them as possible. She has to succeed in breaking free of them for Sadie's sake.

Filled with new energy, she stands and lifts Sadie. The child is light, even for Nicki, who isn't terribly strong. She carries her back to the tree where they slept during the night and lays her down. Wanting to give her a proper burial, she makes a clearing by pushing the pine needles aside, and attempts to claw into the soil with her hands and fingernails. But between the large roots of the tree and the cold, packed-in dirt, digging is impossible. Even with a shovel, she wouldn't be able to manage it.

She moves Sadie to the space she made and places the stuffed animals on either side of her. "Don't be frightened. Becca and Mr. Fluffernutter are with you." She kneels over her and kisses her forehead. "Sleep well, sweet sister."

Beginning with her feet and moving upward over her torso, she piles leaves and pine needles on top of her friend, covering the stuffed animals before pausing at her neck. The thought of sullying Sadie's beautiful face with the dirty mixture holds her back.

A voice carried by the wind distracts her. *Uncle?* She emerges from under the branches and listens. The sound comes again, and this time she's nearly certain it's Uncle calling out her name.

Nicki ducks back under the tree to finish the burial. But for some reason, Sadie's face is no longer visible. Did she fully cover her already? She could've sworn the task wasn't done. Nicki blinks hard, but when she opens her eyes again, she sees nothing but a mound of pine needles.

Her dislike for completing the job must've blocked her memory of it. Her grief and fear made everything seem confusing. But now she needs to leave. Sadie would be counting on her to succeed in their escape.

She blows a kiss at her dear friend's grave before turning away, putting on her backpack, and straightening her shoulders. A new feeling of lightness comes over her despite the weight she carries. Setting a brisk pace toward the east, she pictures Sadie dissolving into a puff of vapor and becoming the wind under her wings.

Chapter Twenty-Seven

THEY COME for Rebecca in the middle of the night. Toth's first act is to place a swatch of duct tape over her mouth. His second is to pull her up from the bed while Patricia holds the pistol on her.

"I think you met my sister," Toth says.

If not for her mindcasts, Rebecca would've been surprised by the revelation of Toth's connection to the woman who waited on her at the local bar and grill.

Patricia gives her a nasty smile. "I've kept track of you through the years. It was a shock when I thought I recognized you coming into the restaurant. I checked your credit card to be sure."

So they knew about her within hours of her arriving in town. That car outside her motel room the second night could've been Toth watching her. He must've known who she was before she even walked into his service station. Patricia was at home and certainly watching when she ran into their backyard and banged at the door of the shed. By then they must've decided they had to get rid of her.

She failed at sleuthing, but she never expected to make it her career anyway. If only she could get answers to her remaining questions, though. The tape over her mouth prevents her from asking them.

Her knees buckle when she takes her first steps, and Toth raises her back up. He forces her forward, through the hall, down the stairs, and past the kitchen to the front door. Outside, her Honda is parked close to the steps. Dread fills her at the sight of the open trunk.

As they draw nearer, Rebecca spots her luggage in the backseat. Toth must've taken her motel key after knocking her out. He could've dumped her back here before returning to her room to gather her things during the night. He probably left the key on the table to make it look like she checked out. Smart. It would be hard to convince the police she hadn't left of her own accord… unless they tried to track her movements from her cell phone. Toth must've destroyed it, and if so, wouldn't it be odd when it didn't show up anywhere? *But it's too late for me now.*

"Get in," he says, dragging her to the edge of the trunk.

She knows they'll just hurt her more if she resists. Without the use of her hands, she has to awkwardly sit inside it, tumbling backward, banging her shoulders, head, legs. The sleeve of her jacket catches on the latch, causing her arm to pull back painfully. When Toth pushes her further inside, the sleeve tears.

Once she is all in, he slams the trunk shut. She hears him get into the driver's seat, start the car, and back out. Eventually she feels a swerve to the right, which means he has turned onto the highway and is heading east up the mountain—just as Martin did with her earlier.

She keeps her eyes closed trying not to think how much

like a coffin this is. The air smells musty and her stomach, though it's empty, feels queasy as they careen around each corner. She only hopes his driving is poor enough to attract the attention of the highway patrol.

Her eyes snap open again as she remembers something important—the hair in her back pocket. It *is* her own car, and anyone might lose some strands bending over their trunk, but if she scatters what she has, it might be enough for police to conclude she must've been riding in here. Anything that might lead to a conviction is worth a try. She digs into her pocket for the hair and spreads it as best she can throughout the cramped space.

Given the length of time, it appears they're traveling at least as high up into the mountains as she and Martin did. There's a long stretch of emptiness before they would reach the ski area, currently closed, and she expects they'll pull off somewhere along that section. Sure enough, within ten more minutes the car slows before turning left onto a bumpy surface. With her banging over every ditch and stone, they wind along what must be a dirt road for some time.

Finally the car stops and the engine is shut off. Rebecca hears a second vehicle approaching behind them and for a fleeting instant, pictures the highway patrol. But then that car goes silent too. As she listens, Toth gets out and walks back to the second car, where he and Patricia share a muttered conversation. Of course, she's here to drive Toth back home after the deed is done. Rebecca figures they'll simply leave her dead body next to her car here in the wilderness. Her remains will be discovered eventually, but if they're lucky, not till after winter. If they're really lucky, police might assume she was stupidly wandering around and got caught by an angry pot grower. Though weed is legal now, she's heard some still work and live in the mountains and protect their property ferociously.

The trunk comes open. A glimpse past Jeremy shows Patricia still seated in her car, her gaze cast to the side like she wants nothing to do with this dirty work though she knows it has to be done.

When Toth grabs Rebecca and pulls her out, adrenaline shoots through her with the realization that now is the only chance she'll get, when he's off guard and not expecting any fight out of her. As soon as her feet touch the ground, she straightens, thrusting her head at Jeremy's chin. She hits it hard, even hears a crack. It hurts her like hell too, but what matters is he's crying out in pain and has fallen backward.

She turns the other way and runs into the forest, her only chance of hiding from them. Her eyes at least are used to the dark after all that time in the trunk. Her burning desire to live gives her a burst of speed, and though she's awkward and unbalanced with her hands bound behind her back, she puts distance between them.

But already she hears the sounds of him coming after her. The next thing she knows, a gunshot erupts behind her. The noise makes her body spasm but she doesn't think it hit her, at least she can't feel anything. She weaves and dodges to avoid the next shot and when a gap in the underbrush appears, she turns off the trail to make it harder for him to aim at her. But then the tear in her sleeve catches on a branch, stopping her, nearly knocking her backward. She yanks hard on it, ripping the material further, before she breaks free and sprints forward again.

Toth's footsteps crunch behind her, drawing closer by the second. The bushes and sweeping branches of trees slow her down, until abruptly the forest opens up and she finds herself on top of a rocky promontory. She runs to the edge of it, barely halting in time, teetering above a sheer drop.

Turning back, she glimpses Toth emerging into the clearing and pausing to raise his gun. The shot explodes from behind at the same second she leaps from the precipice.

Part VI

Chapter Twenty-Eight

MARTIN WAKES with the sensation of a long, wet, scratchy tongue licking his hand. When he opens his eyes, he's greeted by Guy standing next to the bed, resting her head on the blanket, staring at him with an aggrieved expression. *Do you mean to let me die of starvation?* those soulful eyes say.

It's 7:40, only ten minutes later than his normal rising time, but an eternity to his dog. He rubs her head and gets up. "It's coming, it's coming," he says. She follows him down the hall and sits like the good doggie she is while he pours her kibble. She waits for his signal before diving into the bowl and swallowing huge mouthfuls without chewing, like she's in a race to finish first, even though she's the only dog around.

When she's done, she goes out back to do her business. Martin makes a mental note to clean up out there later. For now, he needs to tend to himself. He's hosting an Open House at ten and has to drop by the office for some flyers first. Still plenty of time to shower and dress and make a decent breakfast.

First he returns to his bedroom to check his phone,

though. It disappoints him to see there's no message from Rebecca, not even a quick text. He asked her to check in this morning, but it's still early and maybe she's asleep. He probably shouldn't worry, but he hasn't been able to get her, and the story of her kidnapped sister, out of his head since last night. After coming home, he spent several hours on the Internet reading articles about the search for Sadie. In the process, he learned that Rebecca's mother killed herself. He could only imagine how much that must have torn her apart, losing her sister and then her mother too.

But her actions in coming here by herself were rash, and he can't help fearing she might keep on acting rashly. Without knowing a thing about Martin except that his car was used to snatch her sister, she allowed herself to be alone with him when they went to view the house. She's just lucky he's not a serial killer. What if she's doing the same with Jeremy, who might actually be a serial killer?

While Martin showers, he considers the possibility that Jeremy is guilty. He never liked the guy, but he always tried hard not to show it. They went to school together, and it sickened Martin to see the way the other kids picked on him for his physical appearance and difficulty speaking. A few times Martin got involved and stuck up for him. One time he ended up in a fist fight, for which his father had to be called. But as soon as they got in the car, his dad said he was proud of him for standing up to bullies.

If Rebecca is right about Jeremy, she could be in danger. He easily could've seen her in town and might even recognize her. He might be keeping tabs on his victim's family. Or victims' families? Oh god, Martin hopes there's not more than one of them.

He makes himself scrambled eggs and a piece of whole

wheat toast, and tries not to be too anal about cutting the bread exactly in half. Whenever he's anxious about something, his OCD tends to kick in harder.

As he gets up to do the dishes, the buzz of his phone stops him short, but it turns out to be an unimportant text from his coworker, Luanne. It still feels too early to call Rebecca, so he finishes the cleanup and then brings Guy outside to the line where she spends her mornings whenever the weather is nice.

He makes it to the office by 9:15 and heads to the Open House after grabbing the flyers. During the drive, he decides it's late enough to call Rebecca. He's willing to take the chance she'll be mad at him for waking her just to relieve his mind of worry.

It rings four times before going into her message. After the beep, he says, "Hi, hope I'm not calling too early but I just wanted to see how you're doing. Please give me a call when you get a minute." He hangs up, wondering if he's just ruined his odds of ever seeing her again.

When he gets to the Warrington's, setting everything up distracts his mind for a while. Turning on lights, spraying a bit of air freshener, checking each room to be sure there's nothing out of place. Luckily the owners have already moved out and they have the house staged with rented furnishings. That always works better than when sellers leave their personal items about. Still, there are always a few last things that need adjustment, like straightening a tilted lamp shade and closing the toilet cover.

The Warrington house has been on the market for a while so he's not expecting too many visitors. But the second couple to arrive shows a good deal of interest and plies him with questions for nearly two hours. At the end of this, they've decided not to make an offer, but they would like

Martin to help them find something else. A lose-win, in other words.

When they finally leave, he checks his phone and is seriously disconcerted not to find a reply from Rebecca. *Fuck it.* He calls her again, and again she doesn't answer. His message this time says, "Hey, I don't mean to be a pest, but if you could please whip off a quick text, like even if it says, 'lay off, buddy,' I would feel better just hearing from you. Thanks."

After twenty minutes of still no response, he calls his coworker. "Luanne, I know this must be really inconvenient, but is there any way you can take over the Warrington Open House for me? It's only another hour. I have a family emergency."

He hears pages flipping like she's checking her day planner. She's old-fashioned in that she still prefers paper. "Sure, I've got nothing till three today. And then you'll owe me one, ha!"

"That's right, you can hit me up for something big."

"Oh I will, dude. I will."

There's a couple wandering through the rooms when Luanne arrives so she'll have some work to do after they finish looking. "I love you, Luanne," Martin says on his way out the door. Once he checks his phone, confirming there's still no response from Rebecca, he sets out in his Subaru for her motel.

Seeing that her car isn't there, front or back or across the street, he parks by the front lobby. Is it possible she just went back home? After doing his research on the Internet, he knows she wasn't lying about the kidnapping. But maybe she's a whack job who likes to make up stories about leads in the case. Milking her family history for sympathy.

Just to check, before getting out he does a Google search

of "Rebecca Danser" on his phone, to find out if she might be in the habit of wandering the state, randomly accusing people of kidnapping her sister. If so, she must've gotten into trouble now and then. There ought to be an article or a police report, but nothing comes up. Did she escape from an asylum? Nothing like that either.

The thing is, what she said about his dad's car made sense. It really was gone that weekend. His gut tells him she meant every word she said to him. And therefore it's weird and somewhat scary that she's ignoring his calls.

He goes into the lobby. Richard, whose father is a friend of Martin's, comes out from the back. "Hey, how's it going?" Martin says.

"Fine." Richard looks puzzled to see him there. "You don't want a room, do you?"

"No, I do have a house nearby. I wanted to ask about someone who's been staying here. Her name's Rebecca Danser."

Richard gets a sly look on his face. "Oh the hot one?"

"Don't get any ideas, man."

His expression deflates. "Well anyway, she checked out."

"You saw her leave?"

"No. But when Sharon went up to clean the room, she found all her stuff gone and the key on the table."

"So… no one saw her leave? What time does Sharon start work?"

"Eight. Sometimes she's a little late, but no more than fifteen minutes."

"Is this office open all night?"

"With the number of guests we get this time of year? I go home at seven and leave out a number they can call."

Martin nods. "Thanks." Returning to his car, he just sits

there. What now? She must've gone sometime between the time they left the restaurant and 8:00 a.m. Did she really just drive home without letting him know? Is it possible she has so little consideration for other people, she wouldn't bother replying to his messages? He thought they had a connection last night. Was it all in his head? He drums his fingers on the dash, until deciding to go to Jeremy's service station.

When Martin goes inside, he finds Greg, the assistant, at the register. "Hey, is Jeremy here?" he says.

"Took the day off," Greg says.

"Is he sick?"

"Didn't seem like it yesterday."

"Going on vacation?"

Greg shrugs. "He doesn't tell me anything. Should I say you were looking for him?"

"No, I'll call him. I have his number." Martin returns to his car, shaken. It doesn't feel like a coincidence, that on the day Rebecca seemingly disappears, Jeremy does too. He wonders if he has enough justification for going to the police, then he squelches that idea. He's got nothing at this point. They would laugh him out of the station.

He could go to Jeremy's house, though. What would he say? *I met this girl who thinks you kidnapped her sister. Did you take her too?* But with a little more thought, he comes up with a way to handle it.

Driving up to the house, he parks in the driveway behind a Chevy sedan that must belong to Jeremy or his sister. There's also a pickup truck on the side of the lot. If Rebecca was here, wouldn't her car be here too? There's a windowless garage. Not sure how he's going to get a look in there if anyone's home. Patricia is an odd duck too. Always doted on her brother when he was a kid. Fiercely protective of him, like she was his mother, not his sister. Might be that anything he does is fine with her. Their parents died young and she brought him up since he was nine or something. Like Jeremy, she keeps to herself, but she's always nice enough at JJs. He seems to remember she had a daughter, but it's been a long time since he heard anything about her.

Before getting out, he takes a minute to look around the place. He'd like to snoop around the back, but that might be taking it too far at this point. Glancing up, he glimpses a man, apparently Jeremy, at an upstairs window. The man immediately shifts out of view.

Martin gets out and knocks at the door. It doesn't take long before Patricia answers, blocking the opening with her body. Not that it wouldn't be easy to push past her if he wanted to.

"Hello." Her lips are smiling but her eyes are cold. "Nice to see you, Martin. How can I help you?"

"I was hoping to talk to your brother. Is he home?"

"No," she says. "Can I give him a message?"

Not too smart to lie about it. Jeremy must not have let her know he was going to show himself at the upstairs window. Martin tries to peer past her into the house, looking for any signs of Rebecca having come here. He also listens carefully for any sounds of her.

"Will he be back soon? I can wait." He stalls to give Rebecca a chance to cry out if she's inside. No way does he expect Patricia to invite him in.

"He won't be back for hours. I can have him call you then. What is it that's so important?"

"I have a client who expressed interest in buying the service station. I think he wants to build it up a bit. Add a café or something. The guy seems to have money to invest."

"Jeremy is certainly not going to sell it."

"Are you sure? It would be—"

"Good day." She shuts the door on him.

Returning to his car, he glances back up at the window, but Jeremy is doing a better job concealing himself now. There's nothing Martin can do but leave. He's sure now that something suspicious is going on. Patricia lied about Jeremy not being there, and she clearly wanted Martin gone. And there's still the mystery of why Jeremy would take the day off just to stay home.

He can't let this go. From there, he drives directly to the county sheriff's substation. Unfortunately, Officer Fitzpatrick is at the front desk. Martin has never liked the guy. In school, Fitz was one of those bullies who loved picking on Jeremy.

Martin approaches and asks to speak with the sheriff.

"He's out on a call," Fitz says. "How can I help you, Martin?"

"When will the sheriff be back?"

"Not for a few hours. I can help you. What is it?"

Martin has no choice but to try to explain what's going on. That Rebecca Danser came to town telling him she believed Jeremy Toth was behind the Sadie Danser kidnapping. Meanwhile, Fitz is looking it up on his computer.

The explanation for how Rebecca became convinced of this comes out all wrong. The truth is, Martin can't really remember the details. Something about an informant, but the reason why they waited so long to say anything isn't clear to him, and he bungles trying to explain it.

"If this is true, why isn't the FBI here?" Fitz says.

"She didn't think she had enough proof to contact them yet."

"Uh huh." Fitz looks up at Martin. "You know, you may

think you're another Pedro Pascal, but we all get rejected now and then. She went home. She didn't want to see you again."

"Pedro Pascal?"

"Aren't you Hispanic?" Fitz says.

"Half-Hispanic. So?"

"So, *Narcos*? He played Peña. And Oberyn in *Game of Thrones*. You watch TV?"

"Not much. Look, she might not have wanted to date me, but she was too nice to just ignore my messages."

Fitz rolls his eyes. "This the first time you dated someone who didn't answer your calls the next day? Lucky guy."

"This is fucking serious," Martin says.

Fitz stands up. "You don't fucking talk to an officer of the law like that. Come back when you've got something. This is nothing."

He's only wasting time with this idiot. Martin spins around and heads to the door.

Chapter Twenty-Nine

AFTER STRIKING out at the sheriff's office, Martin returns home, settles on the couch next to Guy, and considers his options. What else can he do, short of breaking into Jeremy's house? Maybe Fitz was right. Martin got rejected and he's having trouble dealing with that. It's true he hasn't been rejected too often. But in this case, there's an age difference. He might be ten or twelve years older than her. Maybe she thinks he looks like an old man.

He checks his phone again for messages. Still no word from her, but there's one from Luanne that he's needed at the office if he can make it. He grabs two energy bars since he hasn't had lunch, and heads off. It turns out to be a busy afternoon, with Luanne looking terribly relieved to see him after trying to juggle two different couples. He takes over with one of them, and it isn't till seven that the contract is filled out, signed, and delivered. Meanwhile he's been glancing at his phone every ten minutes.

When he gets home, he calls Rebecca and leaves one last message. "Look, it's fine if you didn't click with me. I'm a big boy and I can take it. But I'm seriously concerned about you. If you have a heart, you'll take one second to respond, 'I'm okay.' Please?"

Too demoralized to cook something real tonight, he just heats up a frozen pizza for dinner. His phone remains by his elbow while he eats.

It's too much. He has to do something or he'll never forgive himself if anything has happened to her. He remembers her saying something about a detective in Sadie's case who still keeps in touch with her. What was his name? Jeffrey? He's not sure. But maybe the guy still works for the same department, which ought to be in the town where they lived when the crime happened. He looks up one of the articles about Sadie to get the name of the place and puts in a call to their police.

After identifying himself, he says, "I'd like to speak with the detective in charge of the Sadie Danser disappearance."

The female officer on the other end says, "Sadie Danser? I'm not sure who that is."

"You must be new?" he says.

"Pretty new. Hold on, please."

He waits impatiently till her return a few minutes later.

"That was Detective Lazo," she says. "He's been on vacation, but he'll be back in the morning. Can I have him call you then? Or you can file a report with me."

He hesitates. Should he tell her what he knows? But after having tried to explain the situation to Fitz, he realizes how fruitless that will be. At least Lazo knows the case, and Rebecca may have already told him some of what she relayed to Martin.

"Please have him call me first thing tomorrow," he says.

He stays up late streaming action movies he's already seen

before, unable to sleep. It must be two a.m. by the time Martin finally nods off. His phone ringing wakes him at six. He struggles out of a state of deep grogginess before lunging for it, filled with hope that it might be Rebecca. Instead, it's a male voice he doesn't recognize. "Hello, Mr. Ortiz?" the man says.

"Yes."

"Detective Lazo. Sorry for the early call. I just learned you were trying to reach me last night. Regarding Rebecca Danser?"

"That's right. I've been concerned about her."

"Do you know where she is? She left a message for me a few days ago. I called her a few times last night and she still hasn't returned my call."

"No, that's just it. I don't know where she is. And I'm worried about her. She was here in Draywood… to do with her sister's kidnapping. Do you know about that?"

There's a brief silence before Lazo says, "I know something about it. I told her to leave it alone."

"Well, she didn't follow your advice. And now she seems to be missing. I've been trying to reach her since yesterday morning, and nothing."

"I'm coming out there. Can I meet you at your house?"

"Yeah, I'll be here." He'll do whatever it takes to get Luanne to cover for him.

Martin fills the next few hours getting himself showered, dressed and fed, feeding and walking Guy, and doing repair work he's been avoiding at home. At a little before nine, the doorbell rings.

His initial impression of Detective Lazo is reassuring. Despite that he had to leave home at an early hour this morning, the detective is clean-shaven, neatly dressed, and ready to get to work. His handshake has a comforting firmness to it, and unlike Fitz yesterday, he's obviously ready to treat Rebecca's lack of responsiveness with the level of seriousness it deserves.

"Can I get you some coffee?" Martin says.

"Always. I like it with milk and sugar, please."

Once they're settled at the table, Martin pours out the whole story once again, brushing over the part about the informant, just focusing on the information Rebecca had. Recounting his visit to Jeremy's house, he expresses his suspicion of Toth and his sister in the strongest terms. "I'm sure they were hiding something."

"People hide a lot of things, but that doesn't mean they're kidnappers," Detective Lazo says. "Still, I'm very concerned about Rebecca. It isn't like her to get in touch and then ignore my replies. So, before I set out this morning, I requested a check on her apartment. Heard back an hour ago. When she didn't answer their knock, they got the super to open it up. She's not home, obviously, but the apartment looked fine, no sign that anything violent happened there. Her Honda wasn't in the garage, so I put out an APB on it."

"What about her phone? Can you find her from that?"

"Her phone is dead. Its last location was in the vicinity here, and that was nearly two days ago. So starting now, we're treating this as a kidnapping and we're going to do everything we can to find her. If you can assure me she told you she was going to Toth's house, the local police should be able to get a warrant to search there."

"Yeah, she was going there." Strictly speaking, she didn't tell him this. But if it helps get the police inside that house, he's willing to stretch the truth.

Lazo sets down his cup and gets up. "I'll keep you posted."

After Martin sees him out, he goes back to working on house projects he has put off for way too long. The waiting is hard, even with these distractions, and he jumps to answer his phone when a call comes in a little after noon.

"Okay, here's where it gets interesting," Detective Lazo begins. "The judge didn't want to issue a warrant since we don't have proof Rebecca went there, and we've got no evidence any crime was ever committed by Toth or his sister."

"That isn't good," Martin says.

"Sometimes you have to think outside the box to get inside someone's house. You look for code violations and things like that, small stuff, but enough to get you in. The sheriff had the idea to find out just who all is living at the house. They did a quick check of marriage and birth certificates. Patricia was married some years ago, but the guy died young of a rare illness, no question of foul play. However, before he died, they had a kid, Nicki Gaunt. This got the cops wondering, how come they never saw this kid around town?

"Next step was to call the local education department. They ought to know if she went to school, right? They told us she was home-schooled. Patricia filed an affidavit every year, until Nicki was sixteen. That year, after some prodding, Patricia told them she didn't file because Nicki ran away."

"How does this relate?"

"The people in the education department assumed she must have filed a report with the sheriff's office. But she didn't. They've checked; it was never reported. And that's not okay. You're responsible for your kid's well-being till they're eighteen. And it's really questionable when you don't report your kid missing. It makes us think there might be some parental foul play going on."

"Wow. Okay."

"They went back to the judge, and now she was interested. She granted a warrant for them to do a search and question Toth and his sister regarding what happened to Nicki. They're in there now. Rebecca's not there, I'm afraid. But they're taking forensics. We hope to have some clues soon."

The mention of *forensics* causes Martin's throat to dry up.

"Toth and Gaunt are starting to look suspicious enough, I got the sheriff to agree to send out a couple choppers to search around here for Rebecca's car. You probably know, there's a lot of old logging roads. Places where someone might dump a car. They might hope the snow will come soon and hide it till spring. It's worth checking."

"Thanks for letting me know." He felt better with the knowledge that things were being done, though it gave him a heavy feeling to think that if they found her car up there, it was almost certainly too late to save Rebecca.

"I'll call back when I've got more." Lazo hangs up.

Again, Martin waits. This time when he gets on the couch with Guy, they both nap. When the phone wakes him again, he's not sure how much time has passed.

"They found her Honda," Lazo says. "Pilot just called it in."

"No sign of Rebecca?"

"Not yet. I'm heading up there now."

"Can I come? I can help search. I've done search and rescue before, when hikers went missing."

"They've called for dogs. Not sure how soon they'll arrive," Lazo says. "Fine. I'll swing by and get you."

Martin watches at the window and rushes out to Lazo's car as soon as he pulls up. "Do you think she could be inside the car?" he says, belting into the passenger seat.

"If she is, she's not responding. The helicopter's making a lot of noise overhead and she hasn't come out."

"Right." He's too nervous to say much more as they drive up the mountain.

They reach the turnoff thirty minutes later, following some communication with the sheriff regarding the location. Martin thinks he's been to this spot before, sledding with his ex's daughter. But he's not certain. These side roads all look alike, with no signs and just a gravel surface.

A short while later they pull up behind a police vehicle parked next to Rebecca's white Honda. When they get out of the car, the sheriff approaches. Officer Fitzpatrick lags further back, avoiding Martin's glare.

"Hello Martin," the sheriff says before turning to Detective Lazo. "Keys in the car. Her luggage in the back seat. We noticed some hair in the trunk. Like, that's where she might've been travelling."

"Where have you searched?"

"Not far yet. We haven't been here long."

Two more squad cars arrive as they start to get organized. Before long, searchers are dispatched in groups of two, with Martin and Lazo paired. They're given a radio, a topographical map of the area, and a pack with water, snacks, and some emergency equipment.

As they head out, they look for tracks and other signs of anyone having passed through recently. They call out her name intermittently. But their progress is slow as they attempt to cover the area in methodical fashion, without leaving gaps in their search.

"Over here," Lazo says after twenty minutes have passed. He points out a footprint to Martin. "That's about a man's size eleven."

"Can you tell if it's recent?"

He bends down and peers at it. "I think so. Can't be sure, though."

They continue in the direction the footprint is facing. After several yards, Martin spots a bluish piece of fabric snagged on a branch. "Look at this." He touches it though he's not sure if he should. "It might be the jacket she wore the night we had dinner. It was this color."

Lazo comes up behind him and examines the material. "This is definitely new. It would be much dirtier otherwise." He scans the brush in the area. "Looks like she might've gone off-trail here. See… more broken branches."

They push forward through the undergrowth until coming to an open area with a rocky slope. Martin and Lazo creep to the edge and look down.

A body lies crumpled forty or fifty feet below, partly obscured by the branches around it.

Martin feels a stabbing sensation and has to turn away. *We're too late.*

Chapter Thirty

REBECCA CAN'T BREATHE. Dirt fills her nostrils and covers her eyes. It weighs down her body, forcing her deeper into the soil. She's aware that if she simply gives up and lets the earth swallow her, the grief and terror will disappear. *She* will disappear and never feel anything again. Death tempts her by being the easy choice. No effort required. If she wants life, she'll have to battle demons and endure excruciating pain, though she's weak and exhausted and has nearly lost all hope.

This is her state, poised at the brink of sinking backward or struggling forward, when she hears Sadie. "Becca," her sister whispers. "Becca, Becca, Becca," echoes inside Rebecca's head. *Is she calling me toward death or life?*

A beam of light shines over her. She's aware of voices and someone touching her. She no longer feels as if she's buried under the ground. That must've been a nightmare. They've come here to rescue her. She must not disappoint them.

Life is the word that floats through her mind, spoken in Sadie's childish voice, as Rebecca drifts back into unconsciousness.

SOMETIME LATER, possibly days later, she opens her eyes. All is blurry at first, but gradually her vision sharpens until she recognizes the face of the man seated beside her bed.

"Freddie." Her own voice sounds scratched and distant. She has an impulse to touch her mouth but her right arm won't move. She's in a hospital room connected to an IV bag, wearing a cast that wraps around her upper arm and shoulder right up to her neck.

Freddie pats her left hand and smiles at her.

"What happened?" she says.

"You broke your arm and collarbone. You got hypothermia and lots of cuts and bruises. But your spine is intact and you had no internal bleeding. You're incredibly lucky. It was forty-six feet to the bottom, but they think you bounced off the branches of the closest pine tree, which helped break your fall."

She remembers Toth chasing her, but doesn't recall anything after that. "I wasn't shot?"

"No. He had a gun?"

"I wonder why he didn't shoot down at me after I landed. To make sure the job was done."

"If you saw the drop again… you wouldn't think anyone could survive it. And even in daylight, it was a little hard to spot you at the bottom. At night he probably couldn't see you at all down there… Tell me who 'he' is."

"Jeremy Toth. And his sister came with him."

"Good. I needed to hear it from you. They've been arrested."

These words flood her with relief, though there's still much for her to learn. "How did you find me?"

He explains his failure to reach her on the phone, his growing concern, and Martin's involvement. He describes how they found the car, and then her.

"I want to know how you caught them."

"Your hair really gets around," Freddie says.

She brightens, pleased with herself for thinking of it.

"We found it in an upstairs bedroom of their house. More in your car trunk. Just got the DNA confirmation. They also left a clear tire tread behind your Honda in the mountains. Obviously one of them had to bring their own transportation for the getaway. We've matched the tread with one of their tires. And now, thank god, we have you to testify."

"Thanks to you and Martin."

"Should I remind you what I told you not to do?"

"I hope you can understand. I have no regrets. They took Sadie, I know they did. But have you found proof of it?"

His face grows somber. "And now we get to the best and worst of the news. Inside Toth's shed we found an armchair and a pile of dirty magazines. Adult magazines, though. No pedophilia, and nothing else in there. The team went through every inch of it like you wouldn't believe, and it paid off. They found a broken piece of fingernail imbedded between the wooden floorboards. Small, about the right size for a four-year-old child."

She closes her eyes and takes several deep breaths to settle herself. "Has the DNA been confirmed?" she says.

He nods. "It's a match for Sadie."

It's what she's known since she went back in time and allowed Toth to kidnap her in her sister's place. Yet hearing these words in real-time—that there is actual, physical evidence of what she knew to be true—has the greatest impact of anything she's experienced since she began this journey. "Have you found her?" she says, her voice hoarse.

"No. But we've started looking."

He doesn't go into details because he knows she understands. They're digging up the property, just as they did to Reamer's backyard.

"We'll have closure now," she says.

"That's right." He stands up. "There's someone else who'd like to see you. We were told to come in one at a time, and everyone agreed you'd want the update first."

She reaches out and squeezes Freddie's hand. "Thank you. You don't know how much this means to me." But looking at his face, it occurs to her how hard he's worked on this case over the years. She recalls his excitement when they appeared to have breakthroughs, his deep disappointment when leads didn't pan out. Aside from Sadie's family, he wanted her found more than anyone else on earth. "Actually, I think you do know how much this means," she says. Moreover, she's grateful he hasn't brought up the subject of how she solved the crime. She hopes he never does.

Expecting to see Martin next, she's surprised when her father enters the room. In an uncharacteristic show of emotion, he bends over her and kisses her cheek, brushing her hair back from her forehead. His eyes brim with tears. "How do you feel?"

"I'm okay. They must've pumped me full of painkiller."

He sits beside her, lifts her left hand and kisses it. "You had me so worried."

"Did Freddie call you?"

"Martin. It's in the news now too. Sadie's kidnappers found at last. How did you do it?"

"I can't explain. I'm sorry. It just is."

"I should tell you that you never should've done this. You could've gotten yourself killed and then…" He breathes out heavily.

"But you know you would've done exactly the same as me, if you could've."

He nods. A tear slips from his eye and runs down his cheek. He kisses her hand again. "You saved us, Rebecca. We can find peace now. At least a semblance of it."

"I love you, Dad."

"I love you so much, baby. Forgive me for the way I've been."

They sit together a while longer, content to be together, understanding each other's feelings in a way that no one else would.

Eventually he gets up. "I don't want to tire you. There's one more person who wants to see you, unless you need to sleep."

"I can last a little longer," she says.

He kisses her cheek once more. "I'll be back tomorrow."

Martin appears shortly after her father leaves, and she takes his hand when he sits down. "I'm told I have you to thank for saving me."

"I was worried. You didn't seem like the type to just disappear like that. I guess I have a big enough ego to think our date went well."

"It went extremely well. You're right, I never would've run out on you like that." Her eyes grow moist. "But, man, one date with me and you get thrown into a ton of crap you don't need. I'm so sorry."

"I'm not. I mean, of course I'm sorry for what happened to you. But not sorry for my involvement. When we found you… okay, that was the hardest part. It looked like you were dead. It was a long drop and I couldn't imagine you surviving it. I feel like I went through some dark shit for the next hour or however long it took for the medics to reach you and shout out that you were still alive."

She squeezes his hand, so grateful for Martin's friendship.

"And look at you now. You're going to be fine. You are one tough lady."

"Never thought of myself that way."

"Most of all, I'm happy for you. At least, happy for the closure. I hope it'll bring you some peace."

"Thank you." She keeps her hand inside his. She barely knows this man and yet it feels right.

His phone buzzes, and after checking who's calling, he says, "I better get this." After a few seconds, he hands his phone to her. "Detective Lazo wants to talk to you."

"Guess I need a new phone." She takes his. "Hi Freddie. Didn't we just talk?"

The tears return as she listens to his report. There's concern in Martin's eyes when she hangs up. "He just heard from the team at the house," Rebecca tells him. "They found a burial site. The remains of a small child."

Martin leans his head gently against hers while she weeps.

Chapter Thirty-One

NICKI IS WORKING at Park's Organic Produce stand at the Ferry Building in San Francisco when she picks up a newspaper left by her last customer to put in the recycle bin. Her heart skips a beat as she glances down at the front page. A beautiful photograph depicts four-year-old Sadie, her eyes sparkling and face beaming in a way they never would again after she was taken from her home. The headline says, *Kidnappers Arrested in Draywood, CA*, and the first paragraph identifies Uncle and Mother as the kidnappers in question.

In between waiting on other customers, Nicki reads the rest of the article, which states that police have discovered a child's body buried in the backyard. Although this might refer to where she left Sadie in the woods behind the house, she isn't sure a covering of leaves and pine needles would be considered a *burial.* More likely this meant Uncle had found her under the tree and moved her closer to home. If so, she prays he laid Becca the rabbit and Mr. Fluffernutter to rest beside her. Sadie would not have wanted to be alone.

As soon as the body was discovered, the article says, Mother and Uncle were charged with murder in addition to kidnapping. Of course, Nicki knows they didn't strictly-speaking murder her, but in the years following her escape, she's come to believe that the responsibility for Sadie's death rests on their shoulders. Nicki has learned so much about how the world works since then, including how they were abusive parents and how they had no right to imprison Sadie—and her —as they did. But still she resisted going to the police, because there had been a time when she loved and relied on Mother and she had not wanted her to go to jail for her crimes. Besides, turning in Mother and Uncle would not bring Sadie back.

One part that interests Nicki more than the rest is the mention of Sadie's sister, Rebecca. Apparently she was the one who somehow figured out where Sadie had been taken, though the article doesn't explain how. The worst thing is they tried to kill her to keep her from telling anyone what she knew. But she survived and is going to be all right, thank god. Otherwise Nicki would blame herself for not turning in Mother and Uncle long ago.

Toward the end of the article, Nicki is surprised to find a mention of herself. It says Mother told the Department of Education that her daughter Nicki Gaunt ran away from home at age sixteen. However, since Mother never reported this to the police, and since no one knows anything about Nicki or where she might have gone, there's speculation that maybe she was also murdered and buried out back some-where. The FBI are still searching.

She probably ought to contact the police and let them know she's alive. But what Mother and Uncle did to Rebecca has made her angry, and removed any motivation she might've felt to come forward and at least clear up the speculation regarding the possible killing of their daughter.

When it's time to close up the stand, she has to put off thinking about the matter for a while longer. But later when she returns to the homeless shelter, she thinks of Rebecca again. When she and Sadie ran away, Nicki had been planning to bring her back to her family. But after Sadie died, Nicki couldn't bear the thought of going to them and delivering such awful news. That was when she did not want to be responsible for Mother and Uncle going to prison as well.

But now, with them already arrested, and with Sadie's death being public knowledge, it seems the least she can do is go to Rebecca and tell her what really happened. It might comfort her to know her sister died quickly and without suffering. It's also possible Rebecca will blame Nicki, since she's the one who coerced Sadie into leaving, and maybe she would've recovered from her illness if they had stayed. But Nicki is older, stronger, and wiser now than she was then, and she thinks she can face Rebecca's anger if it comes to that. She owes it to Sadie to tell the rest of the story and let her sister know how she named her favorite stuffed rabbit after her, along with how brave she was right up to the end.

Nicki gets out her favorite possession, something she was finally able to afford after she started working—her smart phone. For someone who was isolated for the first sixteen years of her life, it's incredible to feel as if she's now connected to the entire world.

She needs to call Chelsey Heffron and ask to borrow her car. Chelsey is the saint-slash-social worker who plucked her out of Golden Gate Park, where she was living with other homeless people the first couple of years after she arrived in San Francisco. Chelsey arranged the bedroom at the shelter for Nicki, she found her the job at the produce stand, she helped her sign up for classes at the community college, and she told her how to get a driver's license using her birth certificate.

But before Nicki can make the call, a knock comes at her door.

"Nicki, it's me," Chelsey says.

She lets her in. "I was just about to call you."

Chelsey rushes forward and wraps Nicki in a tight embrace. "Oh sweetie, are you all right?"

"What do you mean?"

Chelsey draws back to scrutinize her face. "Did you see the news? I'm so, so sorry."

Oddly, Nicki hadn't even thought about her friends recognizing her name in the paper. She sits on the bed while Chelsey settles on the chair across from her.

"That's your mother, right? And your uncle?"

"Yeah, it's them."

"Did they really do that? I mean, obviously you're alive, so that part is wrong."

"They took Sadie," Nicki says. "But they didn't kill her. Not directly, anyway."

"Oh god. Do you still love them? Are you going to try to help them?"

Nicki lowers her gaze. "They've done terrible things. You read how they tried to kill Sadie's sister?"

"Fuck yeah. I can understand why you ran away now."

"It was crazy. You can't even imagine. I was a prisoner in their house."

Chelsey moves beside her on the bed and rubs her back. "Thank god you escaped. You did the right thing coming here. You've got a real life now."

"I have to go back."

"Go back? I mean, sure, you need to let the cops know you're alive. You don't want them wasting their time digging up the neighborhood looking for your body. And that's one crime your mother and her brother definitely didn't commit. But you can talk to the cops here. I'll go with you. You don't need to go back there. God no."

"Actually, I'm going to see Sadie's sister. She's in the hospital there. I need to tell her what happened, face to face. Before I talk to the police. I want her to hear it from me first."

Chelsey looks at her, thinking about it. "You're right, sweetie. Poor thing, losing her sister like that. And then, like, all these years go by, and she never gave up hope. She deserves to hear about her sister from you. Do you want me to come? I might be able to arrange it."

Nicki shakes her head. "I have to do this myself. I can handle it."

Chelsey removes her keys from her pocket. "Take my car. I'm not leaving the city for the next week. Take as long as you need. And call me if you change your mind and need help."

After Chelsey leaves, Nicki calls a classmate of hers, asking if she'll let her know about any new assignments that come up. She'll have to miss classes tomorrow, and maybe the day after that, so she spends the rest of the evening after dinner getting ahead in her homework. If there's one thing she learned to do well before she ran away, it's studying by herself. Her dream is to transfer to a real university next year, and get a scholarship if she can. She wants to fulfill her promise to Sadie and become a doctor someday.

She sleeps fitfully during the night and wakes early to set out. Her feelings of anxiety continue during the drive, growing more intense the closer she gets to her destination. Clearly she underestimated how it would make her feel to return to the place where she spent her miserable childhood. It's like journeying into a dark and terrifying cave, knowing that there's a monster at the end of it.

The only way she can force herself to keep going is to continually remind herself she isn't going to the house. She will never go there again, not ever. Not inside its dreary, suffocating rooms. Not outside with its clawing trees and stacks of hacked up wood. And never, never, never inside the shed. Now that Mother and Uncle are arrested, there is no one to make her.

Thankfully, the hospital is in Yellerton, lower down the mountain, so she doesn't even have to drive past Draywood. She doesn't associate Yellerton with past memories. Maybe Mother came here when she was so ill on the day Nicki and Sadie ran away, but if so, that was a long time ago and no one would remember.

After parking the car and getting out, she pauses for a moment staring at the building. A shiver runs through her and she hugs herself. It's going to be harder than she thought facing Sadie's sister. Her right hand shakes holding her purse, as it sometimes does when she's nervous.

She won't let herself turn back, though. One foot in front of the other, just as she made herself do after Sadie died and she kept walking and walking until, days later, she came to a bus station. That taught her she has a steely determination inside when she needs it.

At the front desk they try to send her away. They think she is a reporter pretending to be a friend. Apparently actual reporters have been doing this already. But finally she gets a nice nurse to agree to tell Rebecca that Nicki, a friend of

Sadie's, is here to see her. A few minutes later the nurse returns and leads her to the room.

The sight of Rebecca fills her with a powerful rush of emotions. Probably because of her resemblance to Sadie, Nicki's heart goes out to her instantly.

Rebecca is drinking from a glass of water when she enters. But at the moment she sets down her glass and looks up at Nicki, her face transforms. Nicki has never seen anyone look so astonished before.

"Sadie?" Rebecca says.

Nicki is baffled. Why would she call her that? Sadie is obviously dead, and Nicki even told the nurse to give her name. "I'm Nicki Gaunt," she says. "My mother is Patricia Gaunt."

Inexplicably, Rebecca erupts into tears. Nicki approaches and pats her back gently on the side without the cast. "I'm sorry," she says. "I didn't mean to upset you."

A nurse overhears Rebecca's hysteria and looks in. "Are you okay?" He gives Nicki a dirty look like he thinks she's responsible. "Maybe you should leave, miss."

"No!" Rebecca cries out in the midst of her tears. She grabs some tissues and tries to get herself under control. "I want her to stay."

"All right then." The nurse moves on.

Nicki sits in the chair. "I guess it's a shock finding out I'm alive. I know the police are expecting to find me buried out there."

Rebecca blows her nose and nods. When she finds her voice again, she says, "You're right. Seeing you has been a huge shock. But I'm okay now. Please, tell me… tell me about yourself."

"I loved your sister very much. I was at the house when they kept her in the shed. I'm so sorry."

Rebecca keeps a tissue pressed to her face. "Please go on. I want to know everything."

"I snuck out to see her whenever I could. It wasn't easy. I was also a prisoner, only inside the house. I wanted to run away so bad, but I couldn't bear to leave Sadie alone with them. So I waited till one night when Mother was sick and Uncle took her to the doctor." Now Nicki tears up. "It was my fault, really. Sadie didn't want to go. She was too afraid of them and what they'd do to her if they caught us. But I insisted, and later I found out she was sick too. She died that night and I buried her under the tree, along with her favorite stuffed animals. She named the rabbit Becca for you. It all happened quickly. She didn't suffer."

"And you… you kept going after that? You got away then?"

Nicki nods. "It wasn't easy, but eventually I got to San Francisco. I live there now. I've had help from wonderful people."

Rebecca reaches forward and takes her hand. "I'm so happy for you. So proud of you. You got away."

Nicki hadn't expected it to be this easy. She thought there would be more blame. More questions about Sadie.

"Tell me Nicki," Rebecca says. "How… how old was my sister then? When you ran away?"

"She was four."

"And… and how old are you?"

"I'm twenty-three. I was sixteen then."

"Seven years ago. You ran away seven years ago. And you say Sadie was four then?"

Now Nicki is feeling confused. Why is she asking these questions? They aren't important. "Yeah, that's what I said."

"But seven years ago," Rebecca says in a gentle tone, "Sadie would've been sixteen."

Nicki blinks. She never really thought about their ages. "I'm not lying to you."

Rebecca holds her hand tight. "No… no, I don't believe you are."

"I wanted to save her. She was the sister I never had."

Rebecca draws her close and tries to hug her, though Nicki has to be careful not to put pressure on her cast.

"That makes you my sister too," Rebecca says.

Chapter Thirty-Two

REBECCA DIDN'T WANT Nicki to leave, not even for a second, but Nicki insisted she had to drive back home today because she was borrowing a friend's car. Rebecca had to be satisfied with a promise that she could come visit Nicki in San Francisco as soon as she was sufficiently recovered. She spent the rest of the day thanking and complimenting all the staff, chatting cheerfully on the phone with her father and Martin, and occasionally humming her favorite songs to herself.

In the morning the hospital releases her into Martin's care. Two days earlier, he refused to listen when she said she didn't want to be a burden to him. She gave up protesting before long, wanting to believe he was falling for her as quickly as she had already fallen for him.

She says nothing during the car ride to his house and waits till they're both inside. At this point he's starting to look nervous, obviously wondering if something's wrong between them and she's about to break some terrible news.

He's fussing over her when she orders him to sit down. "I

have something to tell you and it's for your ears only for the time being."

"All right." He straightens two pillows while waiting for her to start.

"I had a visitor yesterday who told me she was Nicki Gaunt. Patricia Gaunt's daughter."

"Nicki Gaunt? Are you sure? The police think she might be dead."

"There isn't any doubt in her mind that she's Nicki Gaunt."

"She should come forward then," Martin says. "Why did she visit you?"

"She wanted to tell me how Sadie died. She said it happened when they ran away, seven years ago. She told me Sadie was four years old then."

Martin knits his brow. "Seven years ago? She must be confused."

The joy that Rebecca felt upon seeing Nicki the first time suffuses her again. "Her mind is confused, yes. And I understand why. Martin." She grasps him by the wrist. "*She is Sadie.* I knew it the minute I saw her. The thing is, *she* doesn't know it."

Martin is silent for a moment, taking this in. "Rebecca. I know how badly you want her to be alive. But—"

"I couldn't mistake my own sister. And when you see her, you'll know too. We look alike. We even sound alike."

"Then why does she call herself Nicki?"

"They must've called her that. They must've told her she was Patricia's daughter, over and over and over again. She was only four. I don't remember anything from that age.

"But a part of her consciousness was holding onto her own identity. And it caused her personality to split. It's the only explanation. It makes sense that she thinks Sadie *died* on the day she ran away. It was the day she broke free of their control. She didn't need the little girl she had been anymore."

He leans back, mind blown just like Rebecca's was the day before. "Have you told her?"

"No. I think it's going to take time. This has been her reality for many years. She was baffled when I pointed out the discrepancy in ages. It might shatter her to know she's Sadie, and Nicki is… no one?"

"She needs a psychologist."

"Yes. And I'm going to find a way to get her to agree to see one. Maybe a hypnotist would be best. We'll see."

"Have you told anyone else yet? Your father? Detective Lazo?"

She shakes her head. "I think the police and the press descending on her would be more than she could handle right now. And if there's a DNA test, and then they start calling her Sadie… it could be too much for her. For now, for just a little while, I'm going to keep her to myself and see if I can get her cured. Then we'll go to our father."

A brightness fills her. "But you see what this means… I have my sister back. I never thought I would. I only thought I would find out what happened to her. But she's alive, Martin. She's alive."

At the end of the day, Freddie stops by with the latest update. He comes outside, where Rebecca is tossing the ball for Guy. Martin hangs back, clearly wanting to give them privacy, but Rebecca waves him over to the picnic table. "No secrets from you after the hell you've gone through for my sake," she says.

As soon as they're settled, Freddie begins. "The DNA results are in on the child we found."

She struggles to keep her expression blank, and a glance at Martin shows he's doing the same. But inside, she's brimming with excitement, praying this is the confirmation she's been waiting for.

"It isn't Sadie." Freddie waits for a reaction from Rebecca, and looks puzzled by her silence.

"So they interviewed Patricia again," he continues. "She claims it's her daughter, Nicki, who died at the age of four. It happened when Jeremy was supposed to be watching her, and Patricia was at work. Nicki was eating some hot dog, and Jeremy left the room to use the bathroom, then got distracted doing something else. By the time he came back to the kitchen, she had choked to death."

"They never reported the death?" Rebecca asks.

Freddie shakes his head. "Patricia said she decided not to report it because she didn't want Jeremy to get in trouble. She wasn't sure if police might bring charges against him for criminal negligence. Also, he begged her not to tell anyone. Figured no one would use his business anymore. He already felt like a pariah in town and this would just make things worse. They ended up burying her in the backyard."

Rebecca looks down and hugs herself. Sad for Nicki—the real Nicki—who never got a chance at life.

"After the match with Sadie failed, and after speaking with Patricia, we checked her DNA against the child's. The preliminary results show a match. So, it's likely she's telling the truth about this being Nicki. But we can't be sure about the rest. Jeremy has refused to say anything, so we only have Patricia's word for it. Whatever happened, well, it may have been worse than a choking accident. But it's unlikely we'll ever know for sure."

"Poor child," Rebecca says.

"As for Sadie," he pauses, probably feeling puzzled Rebecca hasn't said, *well, where's my sister then*, but there's only so much play-acting she can do. "We haven't found any other remains. We'll keep looking, of course. But her body may not be at the house at all."

"I understand. I know you're doing your best. Thanks."

"Can we offer you some wine?" Martin says.

Freddie stands. "That sounds nice. But I'm driving back tonight. Not much more for me to do here."

Rebecca takes his hand and holds it for a moment. "Thank you. Everything you've done… you've been amazing."

"I'm happy the crime is finally solved. But I hope we find Sadie. The interrogations will continue. Maybe one of them will tell us where she is."

"You won't bargain for the information, will you? Do not, under any circumstances, allow them reduced sentences," Rebecca says.

"No, not a chance. Not for either of them. Don't worry. For all their crimes against you and your sister… they'll spend the rest of their lives behind bars."

Martin returns after seeing Freddie out.

Rebecca's face beams as she looks up at him. "You know what this means? The reason Toth took her? He killed his sister's daughter. He was bringing her a new one. Sadie must've looked like her. That's why they called her Nicki." Though their actions were abusive and unforgivable, neither one had been motivated by pedophilia or the desire to torture or kill a helpless human being. This was about redemption. Toth, who loved his sister, had been trying to atone. It's an emotion Rebecca understands well.

Chapter Thirty-Three

FOUR-YEAR-OLD SADIE LAY on the lumpy bed clutching the blanket and sucking her thumb like she hadn't done for a year. The man who called himself Uncle had put her in this shed in the back of his yard and left her alone. It was pitch dark and there were scary noises outside, like animals scratching and bumping against the wood. She pictured monsters like the ones in *Where the Wild Things Are* surrounding the shed, peering in the upper window at her, waiting till she fell asleep before they would break through the door and eat her up. Never, ever was she this frightened before. Where were her Mommy and Daddy to protect her? Where was Becca?

Sadie blamed herself for ending up here. She had wanted to play with Becca and her horrible friend Mikayla, and after they disappeared, she thought they might've gone to the front believing Sadie would never look for them there. But even after Sadie saw they weren't there, she walked down toward the street, hoping to get her sister in trouble, knowing Mommy would be furious if she saw her out front by herself.

And now, because she had wanted to be mean to her sister, she was alone inside the shed belonging to this strange man with the scary face, and her parents were nowhere around and she was afraid and didn't know what to do. She could only close her eyes and suck her thumb and try to pretend she was home in her own bed, though this thing under her felt nothing like the soft, warm mattress she loved.

She had slept earlier for a while, but now she was wide awake, listening to every sound. She had cried a lot before falling asleep, until her throat was sore and her eyes red and her nose all snotty. She wiped it on the bed covers, which she now regretted because the sheet was damp and gross.

After a while she started to hum to herself. It was a song called *The Circle Game* that her mother used to sing to her while rocking her as a baby. She didn't remember all the words but she could hum it and it soothed her a bit and eventually she fell back asleep.

When she woke in the morning, she hoped when she opened her eyes, she would discover it was all a nightmare, and she would find herself at home in her own bed with her sister Becca sleeping in the bed beside her. But after she saw she was still all alone in the awful shed, the tears rushed out again and she cried so hard it gave her the hiccups. Worse, her throat was dry from lack of water and her stomach was like a gaping hole calling out for food. She wondered if the mean man would ever feed her.

Then a little while later there were sounds coming from the house, followed by footsteps and then voices.

A woman said in a grumpy tone, "What is this about? You know I don't like surprises."

"I did this for you, Patty. Just wait and see." This came

from the bad man who took her from her family and called himself *Uncle*.

Sadie wasn't sure, but she thought maybe the woman would help her, so she called out, "Help! Help me!"

The adults were silent for a few seconds, like they were stunned. Then the woman spoke again in a voice of dread. "What have you done, Jeremy? What in god's name have you done?"

"Wait till you see her. She looks just like Nicki. Please. Give her a chance."

"I don't want to see her. Take her back where she came from," she said in a cold voice.

"Take her back? I can't do that. I'll be arrested. They'll put me in prison for a long, long time."

"You should've thought of that before you did this."

Sadie heard sounds like one of them was walking away. A minute later the door of the shed was opened and Uncle brought in a tray of food. She saw the back of a woman dressed all in black, going into the house.

"Eat this," he said.

"I want to go home. I want my parents."

He left the tray on the table and went out without answering her.

She wasn't sure how many days passed like that. The man brought her food but wouldn't talk to her or answer her questions. She cried and slept and cried again. Sometimes she played games with the stuffed animals, pretending they were real and they could talk to her. She would make up silly names and voices for them, like she was a ventriloquist. The rabbit, which she liked the best, she named for her sister Becca.

One evening after she had her dinner, she heard different

footsteps approaching the shed, lighter than the man's. When the door came open, it was the woman who had been outside the shed before. Sadie had only seen her from behind but she could still tell it was her.

The woman bent down and peered into Sadie's face for what felt like a long time. Finally her expression softened and she even smiled, though Sadie wasn't sure if it was just a fake smile. "Hello, dear." She drew a lollipop from her pocket and held it out. "Would you like this?"

Tears were gathering in Sadie's eyes but she managed to nod. The woman tore off the wrapper and handed it to her. Sadie thrust it into her mouth.

"I don't want you to stay out here anymore, sweetie-pie." She took Sadie's hand, raised her into her arms, and carried her outside. The sun had set but it wasn't fully dark yet.

They went up the steps into the house, where the woman lowered her to the floor and shut the door behind them. "Your room is this way," she said. "Come with me." The woman held her hand as they walked up the stairs and through the first door into a girl's bedroom. It looked nicer and smelled nicer than the rest of the house, filled with toys and dolls and books and stuffed animals on the bed. Sadie would've liked it if she wasn't missing her family so much.

"This is your bed, dear." She helped her get into it, then sat beside her and pulled the covers up to her chin.

The woman had been so nice, Sadie finally dared take out the lollipop and speak. "Can you bring me home, please?"

"This is your home, Nicki. This is your bedroom and these are all your things. Aren't they nice?"

She tried to sit up but the woman held her down. "No!" she cried. "This isn't my house. I want my Mommy!" She started crying again and couldn't talk for a while as she coughed and choked and her nose ran. "I want my Mommy," she whimpered over and over.

When she wasn't able to cry anymore, the woman smoothed her hair and wiped her face with a tissue. "There, there," she said. "You've had a nightmare. You'll get over it."

"I haven't had a nightmare," Sadie said. "You're lying."

"You don't talk that way to your elders, Nicki."

"That's not my name!"

"Of course it is. Your name is Nicki Gaunt. That's always been your name. Anything else is just a terrible dream."

Sadie was confused. She believed adults always told children the truth. Was it possible that everything she remembered was part of a dream?

The woman stood up. "You need to sleep now. Do you like French toast?"

Sadie, in spite of herself, gave her a sullen nod.

"That's what we'll have for breakfast then." She walked to the door. "Will you promise me to try to sleep?"

She answered grumpily. "Yes, ma'am."

"Don't call me that. Call me Mother."

"But you're not my mother!"

"You'll remember soon enough. Goodnight, Nicki." She turned off the light and closed the door.

Sadie put the lollipop back in her mouth and sucked on it. She drew the blanket close around her. She knew this wasn't her home, and the woman wasn't her mother. But she didn't know what to do. She didn't dare get up and leave the room, because it frightened her to imagine running into the bad man in the hallway. She didn't dare do anything but stay right where she was until morning. Maybe when it was light, she wouldn't be so scared. Maybe when it was light, she would try to run away.

Chapter Thirty-Four

IN THE TIME since Rebecca gained the ability to mindcast, her life has changed in every possible way. She's living in San Francisco now, sharing an apartment with the sister she thought she had lost forever.

Nicki earned a scholarship to UCSF and is on a pre-med track. Rebecca's little sister, going to be a doctor. She herself is doing what Nicki did before her—attending community college, hoping to earn the credits to eventually transfer somewhere else. Berkeley if she's lucky and works hard. She's not sure what she wants to do for a career, but it's looking like math or computer science. Just as her father always thought she should do.

Her collarbone and arm have fully healed, though she'll never be a wrestler. Now and then there's pain, but she's continuing physical therapy and hopes it will diminish over time. She feels incredibly lucky not to have paid a much greater price for getting Sadie back.

Martin visits weekends. She has given up sneaking around in the past, having furtive sex and then avoiding the man in real-time. With Martin, she shares much more than just a physical relationship. Since he has the kind of job he can do anywhere, he's planning to move to the Bay Area soon. For the first time in her life, she feels worthy of the happiness coming her way.

She doesn't think she can mindcast anymore. The last time she tried, just as a test a few months ago, it didn't work. It's always been a strange superpower, all tangled up with her emotions. It was as if her fairy godmother dinged her with a wand to fix all her broken parts, and once that was done, the spell ended.

Because she couldn't bear to watch her father wait anxiously while law enforcement searched for Sadie's remains, Rebecca told him about Nicki only a few days after her visit to the hospital.

Together they decided they also owed Freddie the truth, even though telling him meant the news would have to be released to the world. It didn't take long before a DNA test confirmed her identity and Sadie Danser's story filled the nation's headlines once again.

Nicki still insisted the police had made a mistake with their testing and she most definitely was not Sadie. But since Rebecca called her Nicki and made it clear they wanted her to be part of their family no matter what her identity, Nicki warmed to her newfound sister and father as much as if she were fully aware she was one of them.

She did agree to begin therapist sessions at Rebecca's urging, and now, months later, on a cloudless October day in San Francisco, she returns from her appointment and sits down to have dinner with her sister.

"I made real progress today," she says, barely able to hold in her excitement.

Rebecca gazes at her hopefully.

"I remembered the day I was taken," Sadie says.

The End.

Read on for a preview of *Before He Vanished*
(The Killing Hour Book Three).

CHAPTER ONE

REBECCA HAD THOUGHT her sister's safe return would end her obsession with child abduction cases, yet somehow her walk has led her to the same *Missing Person* poster for the second day in a row.

The first time she had the excuse that sidewalk construction blocked her normal route. But today she actually chose this direction, although it brought her to a dark and dreary section of town. The buildings on either side of the street are stark and far-reaching, marked by splotches of mud and graffiti at their lower levels. Trash spills out from alleyways, suspicious-looking characters lurk in doorways, and the stench of urine overpowers every other smell.

As before, she has paused at the flyer tacked onto the utility pole near the X-rated bookstore. It looks like someone produced it using their crappy inkjet printer at home. The black ink is faded, and the white spaces are grimy. At the bottom, the paper has been cut into matching strips with the phone number printed on them. It's an old-fashioned thing to do in the age of the cell phone. But maybe it's only her place of privilege that makes it difficult for her to imagine someone tearing off a slip of paper instead of saving the number on their cell with a photo.

A thirteen-year-old child is pictured on the notice. Rebecca knows his age because it says so at the bottom. He has coffee-colored skin, rosebud lips, and charcoal hair cut close to his scalp. No smile. He looks impatient. Is it because he really doesn't want his picture to be taken? Or he's anxious to be somewhere? Or he's weary of a world that's become all too much for him?

The text underneath the photo says, "MISSING. Ethan Pitt. Last seen on…" a date that's roughly a year ago. The text includes the name of the city where he lives, and an exhortation to call the number "if you have any information regarding his whereabouts."

She doesn't call the number, but does Google his name and the date he vanished. One small news item turns up, reporting his disappearance several days after it happened. That's all. There is no further mention of him on the Internet. No way to know if he simply ran away and later returned home, or if he's still missing, or if his body has been found and whether his death was ruled an accident, suicide, or murder.

Simply no information at all.

Her thoughts fly to her sister Sadie. It was a huge story when she was kidnapped. She was an adorable little white girl. Though they failed, law enforcement put a great deal of effort into searching for her. Local police and the FBI vied for control of the investigation. News services swarmed their family and friends. Until they didn't.

Who cries for Ethan Pitt? she wonders.

End of preview.
Please visit margiebenedict.com for purchase options.

About the Author

Margie Benedict writes emotionally resonant, genre-defying fiction rooted in the power of second chances. From coastal suspense to time-twisted mysteries and sweeping speculative worlds, her stories follow characters who rise, reclaim their agency, and rewrite their destinies.

Formerly publishing as Marjory Kaptanoglu, Margie is an award-winning author praised by Kirkus, Publishers Weekly, and the BookLife Prize. Her work blends gripping tension with deep emotional stakes, drawing comparisons to *The Time Traveler's Wife*, *Outlander*, and the twist-driven novels of Lisa Jewell.

Before turning to fiction full-time, she developed pioneering software at Apple Computer and wrote screenplays that were recognized by the Nicholl Fellowships and produced for film.

Margie is now building a brand readers can trust for gripping, transformative storytelling—books that don't just entertain but empower. From middle grade fantasy to adult thrillers, sci-fi, and women's fiction, she invites readers of all ages to ask: *What would you do with a second chance?*

www.ingramcontent.com/pod-product-compliance
Lightning Source LLC
Chambersburg PA
CBHW060709190726
48289CB00002B/603